Also by Martyn Beardsley

Sir Gadabout Gets Worse
Sir Gadabout and the Ghost
Sir Gadabout Does His Best
Sir Gadabout Goes Barking Mad
Sir Gadabout Goes to Knight School
Sir Gadabout Out of Time

Find out more about *Sir Gadabout* at
http://martian57.googlepages.com/home

Martyn Beardsley

* * * * * * * * * * *

Sir Gadabout
3-books-in-1

Illustrated by Tony Ross

Orion
Children's Books

Originally published as three separate volumes:
Sir Gadabout
First published in Great Britain 1992
Sir Gadabout Does His Best
First published in Great Britain 2001
Sir Gadabout and the Little Horror
First published in Great Britain 2002
by Orion Children's Books

This edition first published in Great Britain in 2007
by Orion Children's Books
a division of the Orion Publishing Group Ltd
Orion House
5 Upper St Martin's Lane
London   WC2H 9EA
An Hachette Livre UK Company

1 3 5 7 9 10 8 6 4 2

ISBN 978 1 84255 673 3

Printed in Great Britain by Clays Ltd, St Ives plc

www.orionbooks.co.uk

Contents

Sir Gadabout

To Elizabeth
For all the joy you have brought me

·1·

The Court of King Arthur

A long, long time ago, even before television was invented, there lived a knight called Sir Gadabout. This was in the days of the famous King Arthur and his Round Table. It was an exciting and mysterious time to live in, especially for a knight.

In a misty and remote corner of England stood the castle called Camelot, and there King Arthur gathered the best knights in the land to sit at the Round Table. These knights had to be prepared to go out at a moment's notice and fight villains, dragons, people who drop litter – and generally keep the peace.

If you could travel in time and visit Camelot, you would find the gallant King Arthur, tall and brave, much loved and respected. By his side would be the Queen – Guinivere, beautiful, graceful, and a dab hand at woodwork. Around them you would find all the great knights, whose names might seem odd to us now: Sir Lancelot, Sir Gawain, Sir Dorothy (his name seemed odd even then) and Sir Gadabout.

Now, although Sir Gadabout sat at the Round Table with the best of them, he wasn't quite one of the best knights in the land. It has to be said that he was indubitably the Worst Knight in the *World*. In fact, the March edition of the magazine *Knights Illustrated* voted him the "knight most likely to chop his own foot off in a fight".

His armour was held together purely by rust – and anyway, he'd grown out of it by the time he was eleven. His spear was bent and only good for throwing round corners, and his sword was broken in five places and fixed with lots of sticky tape; it wobbled alarmingly in a stiff breeze. His horse, Pegasus, was knock-kneed and about ninety years-old.

King Arthur felt sorry for Sir Gadabout, who was hard-working and polite. That was

probably why the King allowed him to join the otherwise glorious company of the Round Table.

To be honest Sir Gadabout had not performed as many heroic deeds as the other knights. He'd hardly performed any, unless you count the time when he accompanied the fearsome Sir Bors de Ganis on a mission to rescue the fair maid Fiona from the Isles of Iona. Then he got lost in the eerie mists and ended up in Tipton, some three hundred miles from where Sir Bors was having to get on with the rescue all alone.

Sir Gadabout did once get a dear old lady's cat down from a tree. It wasn't stuck, as it happened (but *he* wasn't to know that) and it only took Sir Tristram three hours to get Sir Gadabout back down again . . .

One day at Camelot a tournament was announced. This is where knights gallop towards each other on horseback from opposite ends of a field and try to knock each other off their horses with long spears. People loved to watch jousting, as it was called, and it was a chance for the knights to show how fearless they were.

A field was prepared outside Camelot castle for the great event. Tents were put up, sand-

14

wiches and those little sausages on sticks were laid on. A row of seats was provided for the King and his important guests. People came from miles around, and soon a large crowd had gathered. It was rather like a football match, with people supporting their favourite sides and cheering or booing. It would certainly have been on "Match of the Day" if television had been invented – but as I've mentioned already, it hadn't.

King Arthur eventually rose from his seat and announced that it was time for the tournament to begin. The crowd grew more excited than ever, and soon all you could hear was a chorus of "Rhubarb, rhubarb, rhubarb".

Suddenly a voice cried out: "Look! here comes Sir Lancelot!"

Sure enough, he entered the arena on his fiery warhorse and the "rhubarb, rhubarb, rhubarb," grew awesomely loud. Sir Lancelot was wearing splendidly polished silver armour that shone and glinted in the sun. Beneath his armour he had curly blond hair and an impressive suntan. He sat up straight in the saddle (even famous knights had to sit up straight) with his squire (a kind of personal servant) trotting beside his horse. The squire

carried Sir Lancelot's spears. It was a glorious sight.

Then came Sir Gadabout – for he was to be Sir Lancelot's opponent.

Sir Gadabout was not in his usual rusty armour, and on the outside he actually looked a fine figure of a fighting man. But on the inside it was a different story.

He had borrowed his brother's armour for this special occasion. The trouble was that Sir Gadabout was considerably smaller than his brother, who was called Sir Felix le Flab. There was so much room inside the suit of armour that when Sir Gadabout got an itch on his knee (which was quite often for some reason) he was easily able to reach down inside and scratch it.

His arms didn't even come near to the end of his armour's arms, and his head barely came half-way up the helmet. The suit was so roomy that he even had his cheese sandwiches (which he was saving till lunch-time) tucked inside the breastplate – the bit that goes round the body like a metal coat. However, it soon became hot inside the armour, and after a short time the cheese began to smell rather strongly.

Trotting proudly alongside Sir Gadabout was Herbert, his loyal squire. He was carrying his master's spears, although Sir Gadabout only had two: the bent one and the one belonging to Sir Felix le Flab which was a bit greasy and tended to slide backwards through his hand rather than knock the opponent off.

Herbert had been with Sir Gadabout for many years and was absolutely devoted to his master. He was a short and stocky young man with thick black hair which came to a fringe almost covering his eyes, rather like an old English sheep-dog. He wasn't very clever, but he had a mighty punch. Few people dared laugh at Sir Gadabout when Herbert was nearby.

The two knights came to a halt at opposite ends of the grassy arena. The squires gave them each a spear, and the crowd chattered "Rhubarb, rhubarb, rhubarb" expectantly. The two horses pawed the ground impatiently, awaiting the charge.

Then King Arthur rose, produced a red silk handkerchief from his pocket, and waved it in the air. The crowd fell silent, holding its breath in anticipation . . .

King Arthur blew his nose on the red silk handkerchief with a loud "PAAARP" and then started to chat to Guinivere about what was for dinner. The crowd had to start breathing again, since they were beginning to turn blue in the face. Someone nudged King Arthur to remind him that he was supposed to be starting the tournament.

"What? Oh, yes!" He was about to hold up the silk handkerchief again, but just in time he remembered what he'd done with it. He hastily stuffed it into his pocket.

He took a deep breath: "Ladies and gentlemen!"

The crowd held its breath once more. The horses snorted and the knights steeled themselves.

"Let the joust commence!"

·2·

The Joust

A cheer went up! Sir Lancelot dug his spurs into the horse's flanks and the powerful, magnificent beast reared and surged towards Sir Gadabout.

Sir Gadabout also dug his spurs in. His horse kicked out its hind legs in a temper and bumped Sir Gadabout three feet into the air even though his armour stayed firmly in the saddle. When he landed he discovered that he was sitting on his cheese sandwiches. It was too late to do anything about it – Sir Lancelot was pounding down the field and getting closer. The crowd roared.

"Oh, come on!" Sir Gadabout shouted at his horse. Herbert spotted the problem and gave Pegasus a crafty kick in the rear, and off the old horse charged. Sir Gadabout held his large shield tightly and pointed his spear purposefully at Sir Lancelot. He felt the cheese sandwiches squish as he bumped up and down.

Now, Sir Lancelot, being the Greatest Knight Ever, wasn't very worried about jousting with Sir Gadabout, the Worst Knight Ever. Just for fun, he aimed his spear at the side of his opponent's bottom. As they came together with a thundering of hooves, his spear found its target and Sir Gadabout shot into the air with a yelp which made the crowd howl with laughter. But even Sir Lancelot was surprised when, on turning at the end of the field for another charge, he discovered a squashed cheese sandwich hanging from the end of his spear. Furthermore, his horse seemed to have forgotten about the jousting; it was craning its neck and trying to get a bite of the tasty morsel dangling before its eyes. The crowd laughed even louder.

Sir Lancelot wasn't used to being laughed at. He threw the sandwich away angrily and urged his horse on. This time he meant business. The crowed sensed it, and began to whisper "Rhubarb, rhubarb, rhubarb," in a worried way when they thought of what might happen to Sir Gadabout.

The horses bounded towards each other. They went faster and faster. Sir Gadabout's armour clanked louder and louder. In fact, Pegasus was galloping at such a pace that bits began to drop off. First the knee-guards fell off, then a shoulder-piece. Sir Gadabout's body armour began to turn around like a roundabout and ended up back to front.

The speeding knights came together with a fearsome crash and the crowd gasped. Surely someone must have been killed?

First everyone looked at Sir Lancelot, and saw that he was all right. Then they looked at

Sir Gadabout and there were cries of horror –
he was headless! Sir Gadabout's helmet rolled
on the ground smashed and dented, and for all
anyone knew his head was still inside it! There
was a stunned silence.

Sir Gadabout's body, with a space on his
shoulders where his head should have been,
was riding aimlessly around the field. The
crowd was still deathly quiet . . . and then two
eyes popped up above the body armour!

Sir Gadabout had (very wisely) ducked at
the last second, and it was just his empty

helmet which had been smashed by Sir
Lancelot's sharp spear. Knights of the Round
Table weren't supposed to duck, but then Sir
Gadabout did a lot of things that knights of the
Round Table weren't supposed to do.
Anyway, everyone was relieved to see him
alive and well.

By this time Pegasus had had enough. The
old horse sat down on the ground and refused
to budge. Sir Gadabout talked, begged,
shouted and even tweaked its ears; but Pegasus
wouldn't move.

So the two knights had to finish the fight on foot. They drew their huge swords and advanced on each other. Sir Gadabout thought he might try to frighten Sir Lancelot. He took up a menacing stance and waved his sword in the air, shouting "HUZZAH!" in a loud voice. Sir Lancelot promptly swished his sword and lopped Sir Gadabout's left ear off.

Poor Sir Gadabout's mouth dropped open as he watched his ear (now glowing red with embarrassment) drop to the ground. A scruffy little dog, which had been sleeping in the sun unconcerned by the jousting, opened one eye and saw the ear hit the ground. Quick as a flash it sprang up and made off with the ear in its mouth.

Sir Gadabout chased it as best he could,

clanking along in what was left of his armour.

"That's my ear! Come back with it."

The crowd laughed and someone shouted "Come 'ear!"

During the chase, more armour fell off: nuts, bolts and elbow-protectors. The dog heard the crowd's laughter and realised he'd done something clever. He turned and ran towards the cheering faces with his tail wagging. Sir Gadabout turned too, but his armour stayed in the same place and he fell over backwards . . . or perhaps it was forwards.

Meanwhile the dog dropped the ear and circled it frantically, barking to make sure it didn't try to escape. He was showing off really, but as he'd never had so many people watching him before perhaps it was excusable.

Eventually Sir Gadabout caught up and snatched his ear back. The dog promptly bit him on the ankle and ran away. Sir Gadabout felt a hand on his shoulder. It was King Arthur.

"Never mind, Gads"

"Pardon?" said Sir Gadabout (King Arthur was talking to the side without an ear).

"I said 'never mind'."

"Pardon?"

This time the King leaned forward and

addressed his remarks to the ear in Sir Gadabout's hand.

"I'll get Merlin the Wizard to stick it back on
for you."

"Thank you, my Lord," replied Sir Gadabout, bowing. His other shoulder-protector
fell off and caught the king a smarting blow on
the shin.

"Hmm, we shall also have to see about
getting you some decent armour."

Just then Queen Guinivere arrived and Sir
Gadabout immediately began to blush bright
red. Guinivere was the most beautiful woman

he had ever seen and he always blushed when she looked at him. Sometimes he dreamt of rescuing her from some terrible danger. Even *he* knew that he wasn't the best knight in the world, but for Guinivere he would overcome all obstacles, face any danger, and somehow triumph. Perhaps then people wouldn't laugh at him the way they seemed to now.

"I do hope you're not hurt, Gads," said Guinivere kindly. She never laughed at him, and she had been the only one to ask if he was all right.

"I'm quite well, Your Majesty – er, except a little trouble with my ear."

Guinivere turned to her husband, "Merlin will see to it won't he?"

"Yes, dear."

"Right away?"

"Yes, dear."

He summoned Herbert the squire and told him to take Sir Gadabout to Merlin's cottage without delay.

Little did any of them know that this would be the beginning of an adventure; a quest that would have tested the courage and cunning of the World's Greatest Knight. Quite how the Worst Knight was going to cope was another matter entirely . . .

·3·

Merlin

Sir Gadabout and Herbert left the vast walls of Camelot behind them and followed a path deep into Willow Wood where Merlin's cottage lay. It wasn't far from the castle, but hidden in the shade of the thickly crowded trees and undergrowth it was like being in another world. They stopped outside a rickety garden gate and looked up the garden path to a small, ramshackle old cottage with a thatched roof and crooked chimney.

"That's where Merlin lives," said Herbert.

Sir Gadabout looked at the grimy, dusty windows and wondered nervously what lay behind them. The old wizard kept to himself most of the time and Sir Gadabout had never met him – but he had heard many strange stories . . .

He noticed a sign nailed lopsidedly to the garden gate. It said:

BEWARE OF THE TURTLE

"Strange," muttered Sir Gadabout. Slowly, he opened the gate. It made a loud creaking sound. An owl, disturbed by the noise, suddenly shot out of a tree, circled their heads three times and flew away.

"Come along then," said Sir Gadabout to Herbert.

"W-well . . . I'm not sure if a squire is allowed into a wizard's house, sir . . . "

Sir Gadabout was certainly not going by himself and said jovially, "Oh, it will be quite all right."

They walked down the garden path. Neither could see any sign of the turtle they were supposed to beware of – nor could they imagine how a turtle could be a danger to anyone.

A little gold knob by the side of the door had a sign above it saying "PULL". Sir Gadabout told Herbert to give it a tug. He did, and the knob came away in his hand. The end that had been in the wall was shaped like a hammer, and engraved on it was the word "KNOCK". So Herbert knocked on the door with the hammer.

At that moment there was a rustle of leaves above them, and Sir Gadabout expected to see another owl fly out of the tree. Instead, a large turtle leapt from a branch a full thirty feet from the ground.

It dived right at Herbert, shouting, "GERONIMO!"

The squire ducked, the turtle missed. It landed on its back with a thud and lay whimpering and waving its flippers ineffectually in the air.

Meanwhile the door had opened and they were confronted by a rather portly ginger cat.

"Come in," said the cat. "My master is expecting you."

The cat scowled at the turtle floundering on the lawn.

"Doctor McPherson – back in your tree this instant!"

"All right, all right," the dejected reptile replied.

The ginger cat led the two visitors into a rather dark room cluttered with all kinds of furniture and ornaments.

Merlin the Wizard, the great magician, was sitting at a large wooden table amidst a jumble of weird and wonderful items. There was a bottle of steaming, frothing liquid at his elbow; next to that was a stuffed newt in a glass case. There was a pile of old, leather-bound books in one corner, and various strange scientific instruments lay around them.

Merlin had his chin resting on his clasped hands and was staring intently into a crystal ball. Even seated, you could tell that he was tall. He had the thin, wrinkled face of a very old man, yet in contrast his eyes were a fierce blue and as bright as if they were lit up from the inside. He had long grey hair, which was a bit of a mess, and a long grey beard. Bony wrists and fingers protruded from the voluminous sleeves of his black gown.

"Sit," said Merlin, turning his piercing gaze on them. "Now, Sir Gadabout, let me see if I can put your ear back on."

"But – how did you know?" gasped Sir Gadabout.

"He's a wizard, stupid," said the cat, whose name was Sidney Smith.

"I have been watching the goings-on at Camelot for some time," Merlin explained. "I have a feeling that something is going to happen, something unpleasant, but I can't work out what it is. I'm worried."

"Could it be my master's ear being chopped off?" wondered Herbert.

"No, no, you silly person," snapped Merlin, who had a bit of a temper. "Something much more serious than that." With that he went back to gazing at his crystal ball.

35

Sir Gadabout began to grow impatient, and tried coughing a few times to remind the wizard that he was still there.

"I thought you'd come about your ear, not your cough," remarked Sidney Smith.

"Mind your own business," warned Herbert, who thought that nobody, least of all a cat, should talk to his master like that.

"My master could turn you into a sweaty sock with a swish of his wand," hissed the ginger cat.

"My master could turn you into a dead cat with a swish of his sword," Herbert retorted.

"My master could make your master's *other* ear drop off. *And* his nose, *and* his eyebrows—" and Sidney Smith continued a long list of things which might be made to drop off Sir Gadabout – it all sounded very unpleasant.

Merlin looked up. "Stop that bickering!"

Sidney Smith went away to sulk under a chair.

"Now," began Merlin. "Let me find that spell to get you sorted out." He picked up a huge old book from the pile in the corner and blew off the dust and cobwebs. The dust flew straight into Sir Gadabout's face.

"Ahhh – TISHOO!"

"Bless you," said Merlin. "Let me find the spell to cure that cold of yours."

"I didn't come about a cold, actually."

"Silly me. A cough, wasn't it?"

"It's my ear."

Merlin rubbed his chin. "Your ear's got a cough?"

It seemed that although Merlin could see into the future he wasn't so good at remembering what had happened a few minutes ago.

When things had finally been sorted out, Merlin came across the appropriate spell in his book.

"Here we are: 'Ears – How to wash them, remove things stuck in them, stick them back on again'."

Sir Gadabout was relieved. He was beginning to think he would have to carry his ear around in his pocket for the rest of his life.

"There are two spells," said Merlin. "The Strong Sticking Spell for brave knights, and the Not-So-Strong Sticking Spell for cowards."

"My master's no coward!" Herbert declared.

A cat-like voice from under the chair said, "Bet he is!"

"The Strong Sticking Spell," continued Merlin, reading from the book. "It says: 'First, the knight must pull out a dragon's tooth with a pair of tweezers and bring it back to the wizard'."

Sir Gadabout gulped. There was a cat-like snigger from under the chair.

"Next, it says: 'Tickle a tiger's tummy three times, pull out one of its whiskers and take it back to the wizard'."

There was a sound like someone knocking at the door, but it was just Sir Gadabout's knees knocking. Very loud and very rude cat-like laughter came from under the chair.

"Are you quite sure about that?" Sir Gada-bout asked in a strained whisper.

"It does seem rather odd, I must say," Merlin replied. "It's written in a different sort of writing to the rest of the book – and where it says 'Jump from a tree and land on your nose' there is what looks to me remarkably like a cat's paw-print in the same coloured ink . . ."

The cat-like sniggering from under the chair suddenly ceased and was replaced by a cat-like gulp.

Merlin's face grew dark with anger.

"SIDNEY SMITH!" he roared. "I'll deal with you later. Now I can see the real spell. It says: 'The ear should be held in its proper place while the wizard recites the magic words'."

So Sir Gadabout held his ear in what felt like the right place while Merlin read out the spell:

> "Ears are for listening
> Don't poke, tweak or grab
> Say these words carefully,
> And stick back the tab."

At that very moment Sir Gadabout felt a tingle in the ear, and sure enough it was back in place.

"Thank you!" he cried.

"You are welcome."

Sidney Smith emerged from under the chair to have a look.

"It's in the wrong place," he remarked smugly.

"It is *not*!" Herbert protested.

"It – it does feel slightly different to the other one . . ." admitted Sir Gadabout.

"Ha!" exclaimed the cat. "It's lower down and sticking out more!"

Herbert took a good look at both ears. "Hmph. Only a bit . . ."

"As long as it's back on and working," said Merlin.

"'ear, 'ear," agreed Sir Gadabout, who wasn't very good at making jokes – but then what would you expect of the Worst Knight in the world?

·4·

Kidnapped!

Merlin accompanied Sir Gadabout and Herbert back to Camelot, so that he could discuss with King Arthur the worrying things he had seen in his crystal ball. Merlin didn't ride a horse, but despite his great age, the tall, thin wizard swept along, his black cloak flapping behind, and had no trouble keeping up. Sidney Smith scampered along beside his master, occasionally darting after birds and other small creatures foolish enough to cross his path.

When they arrived at the castle, even Sir Gadabout noticed that it was strangely empty. "Something seems different about the place . . ." he mused.

"Where is everybody?" asked Merlin.

"There were dozens of knights here when we left," said Herbert.

"Let's see if we can find the King," suggested Sir Gadabout. One of the knightly things he wasn't so good at was getting down from his horse. As he leaned to one side, about to swing his leg over the horse's back, the saddle suddenly slipped and he found himself hanging upside down from Pegasus' belly.

"What a fool!" cried Sidney Smith.

"Come with me," said Merlin. "This looks serious."

They found King Arthur in the Great Hall of Camelot. It was a vast room, with colourful tapestries hanging from the walls and the Round Table, large enough to seat over a hundred knights, in the centre.

But the Great Hall was empty except for two sad and solitary figures seated side by side at the Round Table.

"Woe is me!" wailed King Arthur.

"The Queen is gone!" lamented Sir Lancelot.

"What a fool I've been," Merlin admonished himself. "I should have guessed."

"I – I don't quite follow," said Sir Gadabout. "The Queen has gone where?"

"She's been kidnapped, you nutty knight," snapped Sidney Smith, who had been with Merlin long enough to tell what his master was thinking.

"Oh, dear!" said Sir Gadabout. "Have all the other knights gone to rescue her?"

King Arthur shook his head sadly and told them what had happened. "Sir Lancelot has just arrived back – he was out slaying an evil giant before breakfast. He wasn't here when the old woman arrived at the castle gates. She said that a herd of fire-breathing dragons had surrounded her cottage and were trying to kill her family. I immediately sent out all of my knights, since it sounded like a big job. She said it was a day's ride to the north. When I came back from seeing the knights off, Guinivere was gone!"

"But didn't you see her go? There's only one way out of Camelot," said Sir Gadabout.

King Arthur shook his head dejectedly.

"Just as I thought," said Merlin. "This is no ordinary kidnap. Someone has been working wicked spells here. You must send out your remaining knights to look for her."

"Surely you don't mean *him*?" Sidney Smith exclaimed in disbelief, pointing at Sir Gadabout.

"I can manage quite well on my own," said Sir Lancelot rather snootily.

"You must both go," said Merlin. "She could be anywhere. Sir Lancelot can go one way, Sir Gadabout and Herbert another. And I'm sending Sidney Smith to help them."

The cat groaned and put his paws to his head.

"Why the cat?" asked Herbert indignantly.

"Because . . . " began Merlin hesitantly. He didn't have the heart to say it was because Sir Gadabout was the Worst Knight in the World.

Sidney Smith, however, did have the heart. "It's because he's useless!"

"Be quiet, Smith," commanded Merlin.

"Well, it's true – he's rubbish!"

"I know I'm not the best of knights . . . "
began Sir Gadabout, not being put off by
Sidney Smith scoffing, "The *worst*!"

"I shall do my very best to rescue Queen
Guinivere. I shall risk my life without a second
thought for one who has been so kind to me."

"Thank you, Sir Gadabout," said King
Arthur, a tear in his eye.

Merlin drew Sir Gadabout and Herbert aside
and spoke again.

"There is another way I intend to help you.

You will doubtless be facing enemies with magical powers, so your – er – skills as a knight may not be quite enough. You could do with a trick up your sleeve, and therefore I am going to make Herbert invisible!"

"Ooer!" said Herbert, and he went so pale that Sir Gadabout, glancing at his squire, thought that it was happening already.

Merlin instructed Herbert to climb on to the Round Table and stand right in the middle. Then he raised his bony arms so that the baggy

sleeves of his black cloak spread out like a crow's wings. "This is a very difficult spell – here we go."

He proceeded to chant strange words in a deep, slow voice: "Beth, Aleph, Cheth, Yod . . ."

Herbert trembled as he stood in the shadow of the tall wizard. He kept looking down at himself to make sure he was still there.

Suddenly, Merlin clapped his hands together and shouted: "BEGONE!"

Herbert's left leg vanished and he promptly fell over.

"Hmm," said Merlin, stroking his beard. "This may take longer than I thought."

However, at the very next attempt he managed to make Herbert well and truly invisible.

"W—when will this wear off?" asked a frightened voice from nowhere.

"It won't wear off. But I can remove the spell when you return . . . I think."

"Where should they start looking?" King Arthur asked Merlin. The wizard delved into his deep pockets and produced his crystal ball. He sat at the Round Table and gazed intently into the luminescent crystal in the palm of his hand.

After several minutes of deep concentration the great wizard spoke in a quiet, faraway voice: "I see a bridge . . . then a little cottage. It's a red cottage with a tall chimney . . . "

He let out a long breath and put the ball away.

"That is the best I can do. I suggest Sir Lancelot turns left out of Camelot and Sir Gadabout right. Look for the bridge and the red cottage with the tall chimney. The best of luck to you!"

And so, the gallant knights rode away from Camelot – Sir Lancelot going left, Sir Gadabout, Herbert and Sidney Smith taking the right-hand path.

Their quest had begun.

·5·

The Mysterious Cottage

Sir Gadabout rode Pegasus; Herbert was on his own pony with Sidney Smith riding inside the saddlebag. Herbert knew a path which led to the river Smidgin, and since no one had any better ideas they decided to try it.

By the middle of the afternoon they found the river, and a man in a boat gave them directions to the only bridge that spanned the foaming waters.

When they arrived at the bridge they saw a sight that made them shudder. A huge knight stood in the middle of the bridge. He was clad in black armour, and wielded a sword that would take two ordinary sized men just to lift it. His feet were planted firm and wide, leaving no room to pass.

Sir Gadabout gulped so loudly that a flock of starlings flapped noisily out of a nearby tree. Herbert clenched his hands into large fists, ready to fight for his master. Sidney Smith ducked into the saddlebag, and they could hear him whistling "Waltzing Matilda" to keep his spirits up.

"Proceed no further," the knight's deep voice boomed out so deafeningly loud that the ground trembled under them.

"He'll cut you up a treat!" sniggered Sidney Smith from inside the saddlebag.

"Quiet, fishface," warned Herbert.

"Er, we'd quite like to come across if it's all the same with you," ventured Sir Gadabout.

"No man shall cross!" bellowed the knight.

"Oh, get on with it, Gads. We haven't got time to waste," cried Sidney Smith impatiently. "Merlin would have turned him into a radish by now."

The Guardian of the Bridge, as he was known, obviously heard this remark.

"That cat will make a nice supper," he hissed in a voice that made the leaves fall off the trees.

"Well said," agreed Herbert.

"Who said that?" asked the Guardian of the Bridge.

"Me, of course," replied Herbert invisibly.

"You?" the Guardian of the Bridge asked Herbert's seemingly riderless horse.

"Yes!" replied Herbert, thinking that the Guardian of the Bridge was looking at him.

The Guardian of the Bridge scratched his head, or rather his helmet.

"Talking horses or not – no one crosses this bridge. I am Sir Pas le Port, and I shall slay anyone who tries."

Sir Gadabout stuck out his chest. "Now look here, my man. I have been sent by King Arthur–"

"BAH!" cried the huge black knight with a shout that blew away rain-clouds which had been gathering overhead. "I was guarding this bridge when King Arthur was still in nappies!"

"What for?" Sidney Smith had popped up.

"What for?" Sir Pas le Port sneered. "WHAT FOR?" he roared, making the bridge shake till it almost collapsed.

"Yes – what for?"

"I've been guarding this bridge since anyone can remember. The reason is obvious. The reason – the reason is this: It's because – well, firstly . . . and then there's . . . Nobody's ever asked that before. It must be because – No, that's not it . . ."

"He's forgotten!" said Sidney Smith.

"Have you?" asked Sir Gadabout.

"NO!" thundered Sir Pas le Port, then, "Well, now you come to mention it . . ."

"Then may we cross?"

"I – I suppose so . . ." he said sounding confused.

They hurried across before he changed his mind.

Just as they were setting off into the forest on the other side, Sir Pas le Port called after them, "Hang on! What am I going to do now? I've been guarding this bridge all my life."

"I know what you can do," said Sidney Smith.

"Please tell me," begged Sir Pas le Port.

"Carry on guarding the bridge."

"But what for?"

"Why, to stop people getting to the other side, of course!" said the cat with a wink. And they hurried away with shouts of "Come back!" from the outwitted knight ringing in their ears.

Before long they arrived at the little red cottage that Merlin had spoken of. When they saw the tall chimney they knew they were on

the right track. They dismounted, and Sir Gadabout went and knocked on the door.

"Clear off!" cackled a voice from inside.

"Oh, dear," said Sir Gadabout. He hated to cause a scene but he sensed that the cottage might be important to their search. The beautiful Guinivere's life was at stake so no stone could be left unturned. He knocked again. This time a little upstairs window flew open.

"Ah!" said Sir Gadabout. "I was wondering if–"

Suddenly a bucket was thrust out of the window and its contents were tipped onto his head. It was a horrible green, slimy, smelly mixture full of little wriggling things. Sir Gadabout, who had removed his helmet, got the disgusting stuff in his ears, up his nose and down his neck.

"Pooh!" gasped Sidney Smith, holding his nose.

Herbert tried to hold his nose – but with it being invisible he couldn't seem to find it. Evil laughter came from the window.

"Old lady," spluttered Sir Gadabout, "do not be alarmed. We only wish to talk to you." A loaf of mouldy bread flew out of the window and hit him on the head.

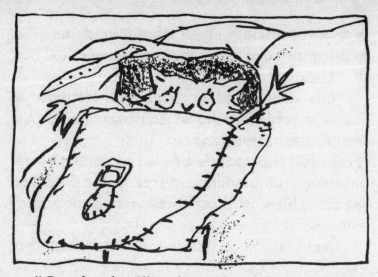

"Good shot!" cheered Sidney Smith. Herbert's invisible hand pushed the cat's head down and fastened the saddlebag.

"Be off with you!" cried the menacing voice, "Or I'll pull the hairs on the back of your neck out. I'll pull your teeth out and bite your nose with 'em. I'll tie your legs in knots. I'll–"

"Leave this to me, sir," Herbert announced suddenly. He had noticed a downstairs window open. He slipped invisibly inside and quickly unlocked the door, letting his master in.

The old woman rushed downstairs.

"EEK! How did you get in?"

She was small and thin, with long straggly grey hair and a ragged dress that looked like an old sack with holes for the head and arms. She had a pipe sticking out of the corner of her mouth.

"Do not be alarmed," said Sir Gadabout. "I wish only to find Queen Guinivere, who has mysteriously disappeared."

The old woman took a puff of her pipe and blew into Sir Gadabout's face some green smoke which smelled horribly like the green slime she'd poured on him earlier.

"Don't know anything about that," she muttered, and puffed out some more smoke – this time, without realising it, into Herbert's face. He started to cough.

"EEK! Who's that?" shrieked the old crone.

"Er, it was me," said Sir Gadabout. "I've got this unusual cough which sounds like it's

coming from somewhere else. I caught it off a ventriloquist."

At that moment a girl came into the room. She had bare feet which were dirty and sore, and she wore a ragged, shabby dress. But the most unusual thing about her was that she wore a paper bag over her head.

"I've fixed the microwave," she said in an unhappy voice.

"Fixed the what?" queried Sir Gadabout.

"Never you mind," hissed the old woman. She turned to the girl, "Be off with you. I told you never to show yourself when I've got visitors."

"Why does she wear that bag over her head?" asked Sir Gadabout.

"Because she's extremely ugly and she'd frighten folks to death without it."

When the girl had gone, Sir Gadabout thought he could hear her crying in the other room. Her miserable appearance had been bad enough, but he was relieved that the paper bag hadn't come off in case the sight of her had turned him to stone.

"Now be off with you!"

"Not until you tell us what you know about Guinivere," said Sir Gadabout firmly. "I'm sure you're hiding something."

"I'm not hiding anything," said the old woman with a mysterious smile. "But the answer is hidden – hidden within walls that run for hundreds of miles. They'll show you a clean pair of heels!"

She shoved Sir Gadabout out of the door, laughing wickedly.

·6·

Castle on the Run

"Walls that run for hundreds of miles," said Sir Gadabout thoughtfully as they rode away. "Camelot's got the longest walls that I know of – but they're not *that* long."

"What about the Great Wall of China?" suggested Herbert.

"Of course!" exclaimed Sir Gadabout. "Off we go!"

"Don't be daft!" said Sidney Smith. "It would take months to get to China and Guinivere's only been gone a day."

"Oh," replied Sir Gadabout and Herbert, looking crestfallen.

Soon the days began to seem like months as they went from castle to castle and town to town looking for walls hundreds of miles long. All the time their hearts grew heavier, wondering whether Guinivere was still safe.

One day they rode to the top of a steep hill to get a good view of the countryside around them.

"Nothing," sighed Sir Gadabout. "Just another castle on top of that hill ahead of us."

"It's on the side of the hill, actually," said Herbert.

"No," said Sidney Smith, "it's at the bottom."

"It's moving!" they all said together.

"After it!" cried Sidney Smith.

He seemed to know what he was doing, so they charged down the hill and galloped across the valley towards the castle, which was now moving quickly. On the way Sidney Smith

made them stop and talk to a farmer ploughing his field.

"What's the name of that castle?" he asked the farmer.

"That? Why, that's Springheel Castle."

"That's it!" said Sidney Smith. "The old woman said 'walls that run for hundreds of miles'!"

"Er," pondered Sir Gadabout as he watched Springheel Castle trotting along a river bank.

"And," added Herbert, "she said it would show us a clean pair of heels!"

The penny dropped. "Spring Heel Castle!" gasped Sir Gadabout. "I just *knew* it. Follow me!"

After a quick spurt they soon caught up with the extraordinary castle. It had stopped at a bend in the river.

Now that they were closer, they could see that it stood on legs. Not wooden legs, nor stone nor metal, but real legs with knobbly knees and hairy shins; one at each corner, and a hundred times bigger than human legs.

"Let's go, sir," said Herbert.

"Wait," said Sir Gadabout. "We don't want to scare it away. You go first – it can't see you. See if you can get us permission to enter."

Herbert walked invisibly up to the castle gates. "Er, excuse me . . ."

Two sentries stood in towers above the drawbridge. One was very fat and the other very thin.

"Excuse who?" asked the fat sentry.

"Me. I'm with Sir Gadabout and we're trying to rescue the Queen. Er, I'm invisible, by the way. Can we come in?"

"Invisible?" said the fat sentry. "I can't just go letting invisible people in."

"It's very important," Herbert pleaded.

"We could see what it says in the rules," suggested the thin sentry.

"That's all very well – but I've never heard of a rule for invisible people!"

Nevertheless he took a little black rule book out of his pocket. "Invisible . . . invisible. It says 'Invisible visitors may only be allowed in on weekdays or at weekends, unless they are Dutch or Turkish, in which case –"

"I'm English!" cried Herbert. So the sentries had little option but to admit Sir Gadabout, Herbert and Sidney Smith into Springheel Castle.

As they walked past, the thin sentry whispered a word of warning in Sir Gadabout's ear. The owner had been put under a spell which made him say the opposite of what he really meant – or at least that's what they thought.

"Oh dear," said Sir Gadabout. "This might prove to be difficult."

The owner of Springheel Castle rushed up and shook their hands (and paw).

"Goodbye!" he announced cheerfully. "I'm not very pleased to meet you."

He was tall, thin and bald, and he wore red and white striped pyjamas.

"I suppose he wears his ordinary clothes in bed," whispered Sidney Smith.

"The Queen hasn't been kidnapped and you don't want to save her. Am I wrong?"

"Yes," said Sir Gadabout.

"No," said Herbert.

"Get on with it," hissed Sidney Smith.

"I can't help you," said the owner. "But first, I don't want you to help me."

"Er . . . oh?" said Sir Gadabout, who was a little lost by now.

"My name isn't Sir Bartholemew the Mistaken. This silly spell wasn't cast on me by the very witch who came this way with Guinivere! If you don't help me, I'll tell you where they didn't go."

After Sidney Smith had explained to his human companions what Sir Bartholemew the Mistaken was talking about, they said to the cat, "Can't you do anything about the spell? You live with a wizard – haven't you learned any magic?"

The cat gave a conceited smile, "I just happen to have a trick or two up my sleeve."

Waving his tail in strange little patterns, he said to Sir Bartholemew:

"Unravel the deeds of one uncouth
Open your mouth and speak the truth!"

As a test to see if the spell had worked, Sir Gadabout asked him if his name was Sir Bartholemew the Mistaken.

"No, it isn't," said Sir Bartholemew.

"It didn't work, you mangey moggy," accused Herbert.

"You are wrong!" declared Sir Bartholemew. "My name *was* Sir Bartholemew the Mistaken. You have cured me of this wretched spell which has made my life a misery, and now I am Sir Bartholemew the True! And true to my word, I shall help you find the Queen and the evil witch who cast this spell on me."

"Oh, do tell us what we should do," Sir Gadabout implored him.

"Ten miles to the north of here," began Sir Bartholemew, "you will find the caves at Crow Hill. The witch who has Guinivere is called Morag, and she has a sister named Demelza who hides in the caves. Morag took Guinivere there, where they're plotting to do away with her unless King Arthur agrees to marry one of them and send Guinivere to live in Venezuela."

"Then we must go at once," said Sir Gadabout.

"You must," agreed Sir Bartholemew the True. "But beware – the old caves are full of danger – and Demelza is as cunning a witch as ever there was . . .

The Caves of Crow Hill

The road to the North did indeed lead in the right direction, just as Sir Bartholemew had said. It took them most of the afternoon to reach their destination, but just as evening was approaching they saw ahead of them many gloomy, uninviting holes in a steep hillside. These were the Caves of Crow Hill.

As they got closer they could see someone standing in front of the caves. A little man in a blue uniform and peaked cap was standing beside a sign:

```
CAVES OF CROW HILL
KNIGHTS OF THE ROUND TABLE - £3
CATS ——————————— £2
SQUIRES ——————————— £1
```

"Good afternoon, my man," said Sir Gadabout. "My name is Sir Gadabout and I am a knight of the Round Table. We should like to go into the Old Caves."

"Very good, sir. Five pounds, if you please, sir," said the man in a very self-important voice. He would, of course, have charged Herbert as well if he'd been able to see him.

"Oh, dear," said Sir Gadabout in dismay. "I haven't any money. Have you?" he asked Herbert.

The man in the blue uniform took a step back. "Talking to horses!" he muttered to himself. "Keep calm. Don't say anything that might upset him . . ."

Herbert maintained a guilty silence, and Sir Gadabout turned to Sidney Smith. "I don't suppose you've got any money, either?"

"Blimey," whispered the man in the blue uniform. "Talking to the cat, now! This man is not quite right in the head – better let him in before he turns nasty."

He saluted Sir Gadabout. "I do beg your pardon, Mr Gadabout. My mistake – Thursdays are free. In you go!"

Sir Gadabout smiled with relief. "Thank you very much. But can you tell me which cave the witch lives in?"

Demelza, who lived in the deepest, darkest cave, had told the man that she was an eminent archaeologist. In any case he didn't believe in witches.

Nevertheless he thought it best to keep Sir Gadabout happy. "Witch, sir? Why, there's all sorts of them in there."

"Oh . . . but we are looking for one called Demelza."

"Ooh, horrible witch, that one, sir. In the cave by the mulberry bush, Mr Gadabout. Off you go – mind your head." He ushered them in the direction of Demelza's cave as quickly as he could.

It was murky and damp inside. Water dripped from the ceiling, and on the ground

there were stones to stumble on and puddles to step into. Every now and then they thought they could feel wings brushing their faces as if bats were flying around their heads.

Only Sidney Smith was quite at home in the dark.

"Follow me, men," he said jauntily. He led them up and down, round and round, until, in the distance, they saw a light shining from a little room just off the main passageway. Inside there was a woman with long black hair; she was on her hands and knees, digging with a little trowel. Beside her was a small pile of brooches, jewellery and coins.

"I recognise that jewellery," whispered Sir Gadabout. "It belongs to Guinivere!"

They dashed inside at once.

The woman jumped to her feet.

"How do you do," she said, and shook Sir Gadabout's hand. "I'm Demelza Broomspell, the eminent professor of archaeology."

"You're a witch!" hissed Sidney Smith.

"My dear cat," laughed Demelza, "I am one of the country's leading archaeologists, and don't forget it."

"Witch," said the cat adamantly.

"If you call me a witch again I'll turn you into a squid!"

"Ah-HA!" cried Sidney Smith.

"Bah," grumbled Demelza. "What if I am a witch?"

"You must tell us what you've done with Queen Guinivere," Sir Gadabout declared grandly. "Otherwise . . ." and he drew his sword out with a great flourish. The blade hit the low ceiling of the cave and it snapped in two. The broken half cracked Sir Gadabout on the head, knocking him to the floor in a daze.

"I forgot to introduce you to Sir Gadabout," said Sidney Smith. "The Worst Knight in the World."

"Charmed, I'm sure," Demelza said to Sir Gadabout, whose eyes felt as if they were spinning round in different directions.

"I am Merlin's cat," said Sidney Smith. "If you don't tell us how to find Guinivere, I shall cast a spell to turn you into a pleasant old lady, always kind and helpful to people."

Demelza screamed with fear.

"How do I know you can do it? You could be any old ginger tom."

Sidney Smith gave her an icy stare.

"I see I shall have to demonstrate my powers by making you rise in the air!" He could perform neither spell, but was hoping that Herbert was paying attention. He uttered some magic words, making them up as he went along:

"Bakewell tart
And lemon sherbert
Make her rise
By the power of Herbert!"

Herbert *was* paying attention.

He lifted Demelza off the ground and swung her round and round until she shouted dizzily, "Stop! Stop! I believe you!"

"Right," said Sidney Smith. "Spill the beans."

"Guinivere," said Demelza, puffing and panting from her ordeal, "is with my sister Morag. Our spies told us you were coming here so Morag took her to – to a secret place."

Sidney Smith gave her another one of his icy stares and began to waggle his tail. This frightened Demelza so much that he didn't even have to ask "where?"

"Morag lives in a little red cottage, near a bridge. You can't miss it, because its got a very tall chimney—"

"Oh, no," miaowed the cat. "What fools we were to follow gormless Gadabout all over the place. She was at the very first place we visited! Back to the horses, quickly."

"What day is it?" enquired Sir Gadabout as they helped him to his feet.

·8·

The Crooked Spear

Sir Gadabout, Herbert and Sidney Smith made haste to the cottage where they had encountered the old woman who smoked a pipe and threw things at them. They spurred their horses on as fast as they dared, realising that the old woman was none other than Morag. They were afraid of what she might do to Guinivere if she guessed they were on to her.

Sir Gadabout now realised that the miserable wretch of a servant girl, whom he had been afraid to look at lest her ugliness turn him to stone, was in fact Guinivere.

Old Pegasus led the way and, after the fastest gallop he'd ever made in his life, the red cottage came into view at the end of the forest path.

They were just about to charge up and break the door down when Sidney Smith called, "Wait!"

He had been keeping a look-out with his extra sharp eyes.

"What is it?" asked Sir Gadabout.

"Someone's coming out of the cottage."

Quickly they hid behind a large bush and watched.

Out came the servant girl, all in rags, with the paper bag still over her head. She was accompanied by a rustling mass of branches and leaves.

"Is that a crab–apple tree?" Sir Gadabout wondered out loud.

Herbert thought that his master must still be suffering from the blow to his head, but Sidney Smith, for once, backed Sir Gadabout.

"It is a crab–apple tree."

It loped along on its long roots, keeping a few paces ahead of the servant girl.

"It must be Morag in disguise," whispered Sir Gadabout. "She's trying to make a get-away – and my sword's broken."

"What about your spear, sir?" suggested Herbert.

"The bent one?"

"Yes. You could throw it round the corner whilst we're still hiding behind the bush!"

"You are not throwing that weapon when there are innocent bystanders like me within a three mile radius," argued Sidney Smith.

Sir Gadabout set his jaw determinedly. "I *can* do it! I've had that spear for years and I know exactly how to throw it. Herbert – fetch me my spear!"

Sidney Smith put his paws over his eyes.

"I can't watch."

Sir Gadabout braced himself, waiting for the crab-apple tree to get closer. He was poised with the spear above his head, arm tensed, ready to throw.

Under his breath he counted, "One . . . two . . . THREE," and he hurled the spear with all his might.

It whooshed round the corner, heading for the shambling tree. It whizzed in a circle

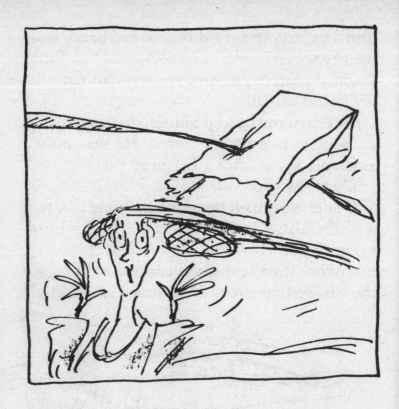

around the tree and headed straight for the
unfortunate servant girl. The flashing blade
whistled past her head so close that it tore off
the bag and revealed Guinivere – much to the
amazement of Herbert and Sidney Smith.
Then the spear circled upwards and disappeared into the branches of a real tree towering
above them. There followed much rustling of
leaves and ear-splitting screeches. The next
thing they knew, Morag could be

seen dangling upside down, pinned to a branch by the spear sticking into the hem of her dress. She had been in the tree waiting patiently to ambush the lot of them when disaster struck.

"Good shot, sir," said Herbert, clapping.

"It was pure fluke," commented Sidney Smith acidly.

"And the way you knocked the paper bag off! You must have suspected all along that it was Guinivere."

"Let's just say," replied Sir Gadabout non-chalantly, "that I noticed there was something

regal in the way she bore herself. I guessed that she must be more than an ugly servant." He coughed a little awkwardly.

"If you believe that, you'll believe anything," said Sidney Smith.

Sir Gadabout scratched his head as he watched the panic-stricken crab-apple tree hopping wildly all over the place.

"But if that's not Morag, who is it?"

"It's me!" cried the voice of Sir Lancelot from its tangled branches.

"Sir Lancelot?" they all exclaimed in chorus.

"Of course," the Great Knight said, trying to retain his composure and failing dismally. "I

was attempting to rescue Guinivere . . . and you interfered."

"Oh dear," said Sir Gadabout.

He was too kind even to think of laughing, but Herbert and Sidney Smith had to go behind a bush until their giggles had subsided.

Guinivere, meanwhile, rushed up to Sir Gadabout.

"My hero!" she cried, and gave him a big kiss, causing him to blush redder than a tomato.

The return journey to Camelot was a jolly one. They even managed to avoid the Guardian of the Bridge; they got a lift across the river from the man in the boat whom they'd met at the start of their quest.

When the little party arrived at Camelot with Guinivere safe and sound the celebrations went on for days.

If you could have been there you might have heard Sir Lancelot telling people, "You see, I allowed Morag to turn me into a tree – a mighty oak, I think it was – so that she'd think she'd got the better of me. Then Gads came along throwing his bent spears all over the place and nearly messed it up . . ."

Herbert (now visible again) could be heard saying, "And I lifted Demelza up and twirled her around. I'm stronger than I look, you know. You should have seen me – well, you know what I mean."

Sir Gadabout was saying, "It was a lucky shot but I knew that if I aimed at an angle of 47 degrees with a head wind of 3.5 knots, I could just get the hem of Morag's dress."

And Sidney Smith was simply saying, "It was a lucky shot."

If everyone knew deep down that Sir Gadabout was still the Worst Knight in the World, it was quite a while before they mentioned it again.

Sir Gadabout

Does His Best

1

The Knights of the Green Cross

A long, long time ago, even before anyone had managed to collect a full set of Pokémon cards, there was a castle called Camelot. You couldn't miss it – it had massive walls and towers so tall they had snow on top even in the summer.

Once upon a time King Arthur lived at Camelot. He was a great warrior and one of the most famous kings of all time, although he did suffer a lot from nosebleeds. Despite what some people said, these were *never* caused by picking, though he did sometimes *scratch* his nose, which is completely different as you know.

Arthur's queen was called Guinevere. She was so beautiful that all the knights had posters of her on their walls; and she was so good at woodwork that there was always a queue of people outside her door with broken tables and chairs, and those bookcases that you have to put together yourself and always end up with one piece left over that should have gone in at the beginning.

King Arthur was in charge of the Knights of the Round Table, which had been made by Guinevere with a special saw he had given her one Christmas. They were the greatest knights in the land – well, all except one. His name was Sir Gadabout. He wasn't *quite* as good as the others. One day, thinking he was charging at an evil knight, he had given a rhubarb seller on horseback a *terrible* fright. And the rhubarb seller *won*. Sir Gadabout ended up having to have a stick of rhubarb removed *very* carefully from up his nose by Merlin the wizard.

He was so bad that mothers would frighten their children by saying they would end up like Sir Gadabout if they were naughty.

Sir Gadabout was the Worst Knight in the World. Or at least that's what everyone in Camelot thought. But then something happened that made the knights of Camelot wonder if there might just be someone who was *worse*.

A messenger hurried to King Arthur's side while everyone was in Camelot's great hall at a banquet in honour of Sir Dorothy (some of the knights had *very* unusual names), who was getting married (to a lady called Dorothy, funnily enough).

The king rose. "May I have your attention. We have unexpected visitors, and though we are in the middle of congratulating one of our finest knights, I hope we shall all show them a warm Camelot welcome."

As soon as he had finished speaking, a small group of knights entered the hall carrying a

white banner bearing a green cross.

"I am Sir Melville, lord of the Knights of the Green Cross. We come from the fine town of Milton Keynes, a place where the ladies are fair and the men are fairly brave."

"Welcome, Sir Melville," said King Arthur. "A toast to our visitors!" And so saying, he and Guinevere banged their tankards together and everyone else joined in. There was a loud crash. They looked round and saw a knight holding the handle of a smashed tankard in his hand.

"My clothes are all *wet*," he groaned.

"Sir Gadabout?" asked Sir Melville.

"Indeed," replied King Arthur. "Have you heard of him?"

"His fame has spread far and wide. In fact, that brings me to the reason for our visit. May we talk in private?"

The following morning, King Arthur sent for Herbert, Sir Gadabout's loyal squire and helper. Herbert was short and stocky and packed a powerful punch. If you ever say anything nasty about Sir Gadabout, don't do it when Herbert's around! But on this occasion he was feeling rather nervous. Not being a knight, Herbert never usually went to see the king alone, so he was worried in case he had done something wrong.

The king wanted to see Herbert about a very important plan concerning Sir Gadabout but Herbert wondered if it was something to do with the bubble gum wrapper he had thrown behind King Arthur's throne when no one was looking.

The more he thought about it, the more he became convinced that he had been found

out. The bubble gum wrapper grew larger and dirtier in his imagination. It grew as large as a tablecloth. What if Corky, the queen's favourite cat had crept under it and suffocated?

Solemnly, Herbert approached the royal thrones as the king and queen regally watched him. They were smiling cheerfully but since he felt too guilty even to look at them, he imagined they were scowling and snarling. In his mind the bubble gum wrapper was now the size of a bed sheet. Corky would *never* be able to get out! Herbert could contain himself no longer; he ran the last few metres, throwing himself sobbing at Guinevere's feet.

"I never *meant* to kill the cat, Your Majesty! It was sheer laziness! I deserve to be *hanged*!" Then, realising what he'd just said, added meekly, "Or perhaps put in the stocks."

Arthur and Guinevere looked at each other, scratching their heads (their own heads, not each other's) and wearing very puzzled expressions.

Now on his knees, Herbert, through his tears, had a good view of behind Arthur's throne. He could see Corky, the queen's favourite cat. He could see Corky contentedly licking a red and yellow bubble gum wrapper. He could see that it was a *very small* bubble gum wrapper.

Slowly, Herbert picked himself up, wiped his eyes, and dusted himself down. "Er, you wanted to see me, Your Majesty?" he enquired casually.

"Are you quite all right?" the king asked.

"If you're not feeling well—" Guinevere began.

"Just a bit of a cold," fibbed Herbert. "I was, er, just sneezing." He did a sneeze, trying to make it sound at least a *little* bit like "*never meant to kill the cat . . .*" but it came out much less convincingly than he'd imagined.

Guinevere looked horrified. Arthur went pale. "I'm sending for the Royal Physician immediately," he said.

Herbert finally managed to convince them that he was neither ill nor mad. They put it down to spending so much time with Sir Gadabout, which led the king on to why he had sent for Herbert in the first place.

"This is a very delicate matter, Herbert," King Arthur explained. "You see, the Knights of the Green Cross believe they have a knight who is worse than Sir Gadabout! His name is

Sir Mistabit. Apparently he got his name from his previous job as a painter and decorator. They say he has caused accidents involving twenty-eight people and one goat this year alone."

"The king and I have never wanted to believe that our Gads is the worst knight in the world," said Guinevere. "Now we can prove it! There is to be a contest between Sir Gadabout and Sir Mistabit to settle the matter."

"Oh..." said Herbert thoughtfully. He *certainly* never thought his master was the worst knight in the world. Now there would be a chance for justice!

"However," added Arthur, "since I... I mean we... I mean..."

"*I* have decided that it would be too cruel to tell Gads that the contest is to see who is the worst knight in the world," declared Guinevere. "I was wondering if you would help us by telling a harmless little white lie?"

"We want him to think," continued Arthur, "that it's a contest to decide who is Knight of the Year. It's a competition they have in *Knight's Monthly* magazine. Have you ever read

it? It's very good! Last month they had free glitter stickers on the cover with shapes of castles and horses and so on. I stuck some on my armour, but Guinevere—"

"As the king was saying," interrupted Guinevere, "we would like to know if you will persuade him that it's a contest for Knight of the Year, just to save his feelings."

"I'm not sure," Herbert faltered. "I don't like telling—" At that moment Corky emerged from behind the throne with a red and yellow bubble gum wrapper in his mouth.

"Oh, all right then."

2

The Contest

"*Knight's Monthly*!" cried Sir Gadabout excitedly. "My favourite magazine! I've still got my free *Knight's Notebook*. I write all my important numbers in it."

"What sort of numbers?" asked Sidney Smith. He was Merlin the wizard's ginger and very sarcastic cat who happened to be paying a visit. He had helped them on many of their quests (being quite clever, *and* having picked up some of Merlin's magic). Whenever he was bored, he tended to hang around Sir Gadabout for a laugh.

"Well, er, six... and eight, my lucky number, and ten's quite important because it's a decimal... I think."

"Never mind the *Knight's Notebook*," said Herbert, who always got nervous about anything involving numbers. "We've got to get

ready for the contest."

"I might win! I've always wanted to be on the front cover of *Knight's Monthly*!" babbled Sir Gadabout, getting even more excited.

"You already have been," Sidney Smith pointed out. "Remember the time you set fire to the King of Gaul's moustache?"

"That doesn't count," said Herbert sharply.

"It was an *accident*!" protested Sir Gadabout. "Anyway, do you think they'll be sending a reporter – to interview me and everything?"

"Definitely." Herbert started to worry about how good a liar he was becoming. "We're expected on the fields outside Camelot in five minutes. Time to go, Sire."

"This ought to be good fun," sniggered Sidney Smith.

Herbert helped Sir Gadabout into his armour. His old armour had completely fallen to bits and this was his first chance to wear his brand new set.

"I dare say I'll be able to buy some *proper* armour if I win the money," said Sir Gadabout dreamily. "There is a cash prize?"

"Whopping big one, Sire," fibbed Herbert. Well, it wouldn't be *his* problem to sort out.

"I want to get something with three stripes down the arms, or a sort of tick on the helmet – you know, like Sir Lancelot."

The problem with Sir Gadabout's new armour was that it was made of cardboard. It had come free with August's *Knight's Monthly*. It wasn't actually meant to be worn but Sir Gadabout thought it was pretty *tough* cardboard and as usual he was rather broke.

"Very smart helmet, Sire," Herbert remarked as he helped his master put it on. He had painted it (and the rest of the armour) an

III

impressive deep blue with his own water-colours (free with last week's *Today's Squire*).

"Do you think it would withstand a blow from a sword?" Sir Gadabout asked.

Sidney Smith guffawed. "That thing wouldn't withstand a blow from a penny whistle!"

"Hmm," said Herbert, giving the helmet a sharp tap with his hand. One of his fingers went straight through the cardboard.

"Oww!" cried Sir Gadabout. "Your finger is in my eye!"

"So sorry, Sire. Allow me to remove it," said Herbert helpfully. He pulled his finger out, leaving a small hole in the helmet.

"Better hope Sir Mistabit's got a cardboard sword," said Sidney Smith with a catty snigger.

Sir Gadabout gulped.

Sir Gadabout marched into the middle of the field, followed by Herbert leading Sir Gadabout's new horse. His old horse Pegasus was in well-earned retirement after he'd finally had a nervous breakdown towards the end of their last adventure. Herbert had bought a new steed at a bargain price from Honest Alf of Diddlem, a village not far from Camelot. The horse, Buck, had been rescued from a travelling show in which he had been cruelly used by a stuntman for death-defying jumps over fire, snakes, and other terrifying things. Herbert had taken pity on Buck. Unlike Pegasus, he was young, lean and fast, and Herbert had soon learned not to say *Jump!* within his earshot. Buck *really* didn't like that word.

What Sir Gadabout didn't know, as he strode boldly forward to meet Sir Mistabit, was that his opponent was not a tall man. In

fact, he was *tiny*. When Sir Gadabout came across a very small person in armour – who reached just about up to his own knees – he said, "Run along, now, little boy. A *very* important contest is about to take place."

Sir Mistabit kicked Sir Gadabout on the shin.

"OUCH! I won't tell you again – go and

play at knights with the other boys!"

"Who are you calling a boy?" Sir Mistabit demanded, giving Sir Gadabout another kick.

"OOYAH! You've got children's armour on. And stop *kicking!*"

"*You've* got children's armour on," said Sir Mistabit, poking his finger through the cardboard around Sir Gadabout's knee and

making another hole in the armour.

Sir Gadabout retaliated by lifting Sir Mistabit up in the air and giving him a good rattle.

The crowd, who had been getting fed up with waiting, were beginning to enjoy themselves.

"*Did you make that outfit using 'Origarmour', Gads?*"

"*Bite his ankles, Tiny!*"

Sir Gadabout and Sir Mistabit ended up rolling around on the ground in a very untidy scuffle, flapping and tweaking and calling each other names, and making the crowd roar with laughter. Finally, Sir Mistabit pretended to give in and walk away, but suddenly he turned sharply and ran full pelt at Sir Gadabout with his head down to butt him like a goat. Sir Gadabout tended to freeze like a statue when he was taken by surprise. He stood, his feet rooted to the spot and his mouth hanging open as Sir Mistabit rushed towards him.

Just as the crowd expected an almighty collision, Sir Mistabit charged right through Sir Gadabout's trembling legs, under a table with some drinks on it, and finally rammed his helmet against the bottom of a three-legged

goat which had been happily munching grass.

"*Ooooh!*" cried the crowd, who quite liked goats.

Lucky the goat wasn't just any goat. She was a Pyrenean mountain goat and the mascot of the Knights of the Green Cross. Sadly, Lucky only had three legs. She used to have four but that was before she met Sir Mistabit.

The poor creature gave a startled bleat and

galloped away. Sir Mistabit sat on the grass in a daze.

"Serves him right, trying to cheat like that!" said Herbert, joining his master.

"Who was he?" asked Sir Gadabout.

"Didn't you know? That was Sir Mistabit!"

"But—" began Sir Gadabout.

He was distracted by a noise from the crowd. They were all looking at a scoreboard at the end of the field. It said:

| Sir Mistabit | 1 | Sir Gadabout | 0 |

Sidney Smith groaned.

Herbert cheered.

Sir Gadabout didn't understand. "But, but, if we're trying to find the Knight of the Year, and he just missed me and bumped into a three-legged goat, how come—"

"Never mind, Sire. Keep it up!" said Herbert, patting him on the back and making another hole in the armour.

The next contest was a joust. The knights, each holding a long lance, had to charge at one another on horseback and try to knock the other off.

All was going well. Sir Mistabit had mounted his horse with the aid of a ladder. He had three gingham cushions on his saddle so that he could see over the horse's head. Sir Gadabout was sitting on Buck, quite excited at the prospect of charging on such a fast young animal. But just as they were about to begin, things took an unexpected turn.

Sidney Smith had been skulking around the rear of Sir Gadabout's horse. He had bet quite a bit of money on Sir Gadabout *still* being the Worst Knight in the World, and thought he knew a way to make it happen. Herbert asked him what he was up to.

"I'm just here to give him some encouragement," replied the cat slyly.

"Hmm," said Herbert, unconvinced. But the time had come.

"Right − off you go, Sire!"

"Yes!" shouted Sidney Smith. "JUMP to it!"

Buck heard the word *jump*, gave a loud neigh and shot off − but not in the direction that Sir Gadabout wanted him to go. The horse felt sure there would be snakes or leaping flames somewhere in *that* direction. He galloped wild-eyed around the field looking for an exit. Sir Gadabout, who wasn't used to such speed, was bouncing around in the saddle, holding grimly onto the reins. To make matters worse, it had started to rain quite heavily. It was hard to see and the wet reins kept slipping through his hands.

Sir Mistabit set off in hot pursuit. "Come back, coward! Call me a little boy, would you? You can't run forever!"

Buck, too, realised he couldn't run forever and, unable to find a way out through the crowd, he decided he must get rid of his rider. It was just like a Wild West rodeo. Buck jumped and kicked and twisted and turned, all so violently that it seemed Sir Gadabout *must* be thrown off. But the crowd cheered wildly when it looked, amazingly, as though Sir Gadabout was going to hang on. They had never thought of Gads as being a fantastic horseman. What they didn't know was that the reins, what with all the slipping and grabbing, had now become entangled around his arm. He was stuck!

The judges had never seen such horsemanship. Sir Mistabit simply couldn't catch him. It was beginning to look like 2–0.

By now, Sir Mistabit had stopped chasing and had made himself room for one last charge. Buck was jumping and kicking on the spot, trying like mad to get rid of Sir Gadabout. The horse couldn't understand it. No one had ever lasted this long.

Sir Mistabit saw his opportunity. He levelled his lance, dug his spurs in, and . . . *charged*!

The rain had completely soaked Sir Gadabout's cardboard armour and there was now very little of it left. His cardboard breastplate had turned into a soggy pulp and oozed down into his lap, where it looked rather like a nappy. As Sir Mistabit hurtled along pointing his long lance, Sir Gadabout sat shivering in the saddle in his string vest.

The ground began to shake as Sir Mistabit, one hand clutching his deadly lance, the other clinging gamely to his gingham cushions, flew right at Sir Gadabout.

Sir Gadabout was desperately trying to get his hand free from the reins. At the very last second, just as he saw the wickedly sharp point of Sir Mistabit's lance coming right for

his nose, Sir Gadabout did it.

His hand came free. Buck bucked and Sir Gadabout shot skyward.

Sir Mistabit's lance pierced only fresh air as he whizzed past.

"*Whaaaat?*" he roared. Everything had happened too quickly for him to see what had become of Sir Gadabout. He didn't have to wait long because Sir Gadabout landed right on top of him.

The joust ended with Sir Mistabit riding around the field flailing his arms about in vain at Sir Gadabout, who was sitting on the little knight's shoulders, clinging to his head and wearing only a string vest and a cardboard nappy.

The crowd were laughing so much it gave them all tummy aches, and the scoreboard said:

| Sir Mistabit | 1 | Sir Gadabout | 1 |

"That's more like the Sir Gadabout we know and love!" purred Sidney Smith.

"Just you wait till this is over," growled Herbert.

He was about to try getting Sir Gadabout ready for the next contest, when King Arthur and Sir Melville, the head of the Knights of the Green Cross, hurried towards them looking worried.

"The competition must be halted," cried King Arthur.

"*Awww!*" shouted the crowd, who hadn't had so much fun in ages.

"But— I can get him some more armour in a jiffy, Your Majesty!" Herbert said. "I know his vest's not as clean as it might be but *some* of that is blue paint from—"

"It's not that," said Sir Melville. "It's Lucky the goat. She's our mascot and is extremely important to the Knights of the Green Cross."

"Lucky has run away and she must be found," added King Arthur gravely. "All of our knights will search until she's brought back safely."

"*All* of them?" queried Sidney Smith, gazing at Sir Gadabout and Sir Mistabit who were still galloping around like a circus act.

They were arguing furiously. Sir Gadabout was pulling Sir Mistabit's ears and Sir Mistabit kept biting Sir Gadabout's knees.

"*OUCH*! Stop it!"

"*Arggh*! You started it!"

"All of them," sighed the king.

3

The First Clue

"We must act quickly if we are to save Lucky," said King Arthur to Sir Gadabout and Sir Mistabit.

All the other knights had already gone out searching but these two needed, well, a bit of extra advice.

"We've had reports of more dragons than usual being on the prowl. We've got to find Lucky before they do," the king added.

"There are lots of goats in the countryside around here, Your Majesty," said Sir Gadabout. "How will we recognise her?"

"The three legs will give you a clue," remarked Sidney Smith.

"How did she lose her leg?" asked Herbert.

"Sir Mistabit was bringing Lucky to our castle and she was run over by a hay cart, sadly," replied Sir Melville.

"A very *fast* hay cart," added Sir Mistabit.

"I see . . . I think," said the king. "But time is precious. Sir Gadabout knows the area, so Sir Mistabit will accompany him."

"Begging your pardon, Majesty, but I don't need that overgrown ear-puller to show me the way," said Sir Mistabit haughtily.

Sir Gadabout walked up to the tiny knight – well, it was more of a waddle, really. Now that the sun was out, his squelchy cardboard "nappy" had hardened into a sort of *papier-mâché* plaster cast – the sort that is put on a broken leg. It certainly made getting about extremely difficult. "You're a little rude, aren't you?"

"I'm not LITTLE!" yelled Sir Mistabit.

"Of course not. It's just that everyone else is very big," Sidney Smith commented.

"Enough of this bickering!" cried Sir Melville. "I don't think you people at Camelot realise just how important Lucky is to us. You *must* get her back safe and sound!"

"We shall do our best," promised King Arthur. And he sent Sir Gadabout and Sir Mistabit on their way immediately.

The only path that had not been taken by any of the other knights was the road to

Upper Gumtrey, so off they went: Sir Gadabout riding Buck with Herbert and Sidney
Smith in tow, and Sir Mistabit on his own
horse.

They rode down a very long, pleasant, leafy
lane, until they came to a narrow path leading
off to the right with a sign saying:

PRIVATE PROPERTY – KEEP OUT.

"I wonder who lives down there?" mused Sir Gadabout.

"Maybe they've seen Lucky. We ought to check," said Sir Mistabit.

"That's Ma Rockall's cottage," said Sidney Smith. "She's Merlin's cleaning lady."

"But Merlin's house is all dark and dusty," said Herbert.

"She's a very *tough* woman," the ginger cat

explained. "Merlin once complained about a cobweb she'd missed and she was so mad she shoved him up the chimney and started a fire. He doesn't send for her much these days."

"Didn't he cast a spell on her?" Sir Gadabout asked.

"She grabbed his magic wand and ate it before his eyes," Sidney Smith said, shuddering at the memory.

"Er, she probably won't know anything about Lucky," said Sir Gadabout, turning away from the path. "In fact, *definitely* probably."

He was so keen to get going he was almost prepared to shout "*Jump!*" and hold on to Buck for dear life.

But Sir Mistabit was having none of it. He trotted down Ma Rockall's path. "I am a Knight of the Green Cross, fearless and strong and of almost average height!" he declared.

"Average for a guinea pig, maybe," muttered Sidney Smith.

"Well, er, it's possibly worth checking—' Sir Gadabout faltered.

"No *possibly* about it!" cried Sir Mistabit. "The Knights of the Green Cross— What on earth's *that*?"

Heading towards them at incredible speed

was a turtle riding a black and white rabbit. The turtle was holding a barbecue skewer like a lance, wore a teacup for a helmet, and carried a saucer as a shield with **McP** daubed on it in bright red.

"I forgot," sighed Sidney Smith. "Dr McPherson takes his holidays with Ma Rockall. She used to polish his shell and they became firm friends. And now he gets all his best ideas from her."

Dr McPherson was Merlin's guard-turtle. He attacked anyone who visited the magician, even Sidney, thinking he was defending his master's property. He had some *interesting* ideas on how to surprise people, to say the least – but none that seemed to work.

Sir Mistabit simply moved his horse to one side and Dr McPherson whizzed straight past on his rabbit. The rabbit had never been let out of his hutch before and wasn't going to miss this chance to join his friends in the countryside.

"Stop!" cried Sidney Smith.

"I *caaaaaaaaan't!*" Dr McPherson's voice faded away as the rabbit fled across the road and over a hill to freedom.

"Very dangerous, running across the road like that without looking," commented Sir Mistabit.

"I bet that's what Lucky thought when she counted her legs and found there were only three," replied Sidney Smith.

"The hay cart was not equipped with a hooter," Sir Mistabit responded angrily.

Eventually, they proceeded along the winding path to Ma Rockall's cottage. Every garment hanging on her washing line was full of ragged holes.

"That's funny," said Sidney Smith. "Ma

Rockall's usually *very* fussy about her things being in perfect condition."

Sir Gadabout knocked on the door. It was opened by a short (not as short as Sir Mistabit) but extremely solid woman with arms like sides of beef and a face like thunder.

"Say what you want and quick about it," she boomed. "Got work to do. Wish *I* had time to go knocking on people's doors!"

"Er, have you seen a goat?" asked Sir Gadabout.

"GOAT?" exclaimed Ma Rockall in a voice that sounded like a volcano erupting.

She grabbed Sir Gadabout by the scruff of the neck and dragged him, clanking (Guinevere had knocked him up a new suit of armour out of baked bean tins) to the washing line. "I'll give him GOAT!"

She snatched a holey apron from the line. "What do you think did *this*?"

"A very large moth?" ventured Sir Gadabout.

The others winced as Ma Rockall's face darkened.

"*Moth*, eh?" she said as she stuffed the apron down the back of his neck.

"P-perhaps a s–sort of caterpillar—"

"I'll give him *caterpillar*," she growled as she rammed various ruined garments from the washing line (some of them very private and personal) into any available gap or crevice in Sir Gadabout's armour.

"Try '*goat*', Sire," whispered Herbert.

Sir Gadabout said, "*Gmmpmph . . .*" Then he coughed something with frills and elastic out of his mouth and repeated meekly, "Goat?"

"Oh – GOAT he thinks, does he?"

She took a fistful of one of Sir Gadabout's ears and dragged him like a rag doll into the cottage. The others followed at a safe distance.

The inside of the cottage was a complete mess. Chair and table legs had been chewed, wallpaper had been torn and half eaten in several places; even the carpet had holes.

"I suppose a *very large mouse* did all this monstrousness?" she asked, glaring at him.

All of Sir Gadabout's different-sized tin cans were rattling together and playing a little tune (rather like *London Bridge is Falling Down*).

It was clear that Lucky had been here

before them – but the only way they could get Ma Rockall to give them any details was to tidy the cottage *and* put up new wallpaper for her.

Herbert and Sidney Smith got busy in the kitchen while Sir Gadabout and Sir Mistabit wallpapered the living room. At least, they *tried* to. Sir Gadabout did the pasting and Sir Mistabit stood on a stepladder to stick the paper up – but he couldn't reach the top of the wall. So, Sir Mistabit did the pasting – but he was too short to pass the paper up to Sir Gadabout at the top of the steps, and so it went on.

There was more wallpaper stuck to Sir Gadabout's armour than to the walls, and when Sir Mistabit slipped on some paste and knocked over the stepladder, sending Sir Gadabout flying into Ma Rockall's mighty arms, enough was enough.

"STOP! STOP! STOP!" she bellowed into Sir Gadabout's ear as she held him in her arms like a baby. "I'll tell you about the blinking goat if you'll just get out of my cottage before it falls down around my ears!"

"If you will kindly let me go, madam," suggested Sir Gadabout.

She did – very quickly. He hit the floor with a great CLANGING and groaning.

"The little varmint scarpered about an hour ago," growled Ma Rockall.

"Are you sure it was *our* goat? Did it have three legs?"

"Nope."

"Then you've been wasting our time!" complained Sir Mistabit.

Ma Rockall glared at him so fiercely that steam came out of her ears. "If you don't teach your son some manners," she said to Sir Gad-about, "*I'll* waste his time all right . . ." and she rolled her sleeves up even higher – as far as her muscles would allow.

"*Son!*" chortled Sidney Smith.

Ma Rockall gave *him* such a look that his whiskers wilted and he slunk behind Herbert and kept quiet.

"Our goat has three legs," Sir Gadabout explained.

Ma Rockall went into her kitchen and opened the fridge door. "The little cottage-wrecker jumped onto the table to get at some food. My carving knife was on the table – and it's *very* sharp . . ." She pulled from the fridge what looked very much like a goat's leg.

"DINNER!" she cried.

"Now Lucky's only got *two* legs!" said Herbert. "Which way did she go?"

"She went over Clay Hill and headed north."

"B-but that's towards the *Dragon Zone!*" gasped Sir Gadabout.

"Forward!" cried Sir Mistabit, marching to the door.

"B–but *fire* . . . and *claws*. . . and great big—"

"Scared?" asked Sir Mistabit, already outside.

"No, he's not!" answered Herbert, gently pushing his trembling master out.

"We're all dead men," muttered Sidney Smith as he followed them to the wildest and most dangerous place in the whole country.

4

Hot Work

The Dragon Zone was cold and bleak and stretched for miles and miles. Nobody (except dragons) lived there. One moment it could be clear, the next you could be engulfed in thick fog and completely lost. Or you might step into a treacherous bog from which it was almost impossible to escape. There were strange noises, like whimpering and teeth chattering – but since these came from Sir Gadabout perhaps they didn't count.

As if all that wasn't bad enough, around every corner there was the chance that they would encounter a *dragon*. Dragons have almost died out now, except in parts of Surrey, and even they tend to be a lot smaller and no longer breathe fire, due to Health and Safety regulations.

In Sir Gadabout's time dragons were as big

as a Tyrannosaurus Rex dinosaur. They were covered in scales as tough as steel, had huge sharp teeth and tails that, with one careless flick, could knock you into outer space.

"Right, there's no sign of Lucky here," said Sir Gadabout after almost one-and-a-half minutes. "We'd better go home for dinner."

"Knights of the Green Cross don't go home for dinner when they're on an important quest," said Sir Mistabit.

"Neither do we," said Sir Gadabout. "I just thought *you* might be hungry."

"Knights of Camelot don't even go home for *tea*!" declared Herbert, and immediately began to wonder if he'd overdone it. He was feeling a little peckish.

Sir Gadabout looked perturbed. "Well, let's not get carried away. We shall see— **DRAGON**!!!" He galloped off at full speed, emitting a strange, high-pitched wail.

The others spun round to see what had alarmed him. The fat hedgehog trundling across the field in front of them didn't *seem* to be breathing fire. By the time they had fetched Sir Gadabout back from several fields away, the hedgehog had gone and they had a

hard job convincing him it had only been a hedgehog.

"It was *enormous*!" he said.

Sir Mistabit was sympathetic for a change. "It *did* come up to a man's knees, I must admit."

"Anyway," added Sir Gadabout, "I wasn't running away. I was investigating dragon footprints. They looked pretty fresh to me."

At first they didn't believe him but it

turned out that he *had* stumbled on dragon tracks.

The footprints in the mud were nearly a metre long, if you included the imprints of the sharp claws.

"Just because it's got big feet, it doesn't mean the dragon itself is all *that* big . . . does it?" asked Sir Gadabout nervously.

"Big enough to fry *you* up a treat," said Sidney Smith from the safety of Herbert's saddlebag. Being a rather lazy cat, this was how he usually travelled when they were on one of their missions.

Herbert tried to cheer his master up. "I once had a lovely little puppy. *He* had very big feet!"

"Wasn't that the one which grew into the Irish Wolfhound and ate the postman?" asked Sidney Smith.

"Can't remember," replied Herbert defensively.

Sir Gadabout began to feel rather faint. He felt even worse when they found some bones by the side of the track.

"The work of a dragon, definitely," decided Sir Mistabit.

Then they saw scorch marks on some

rocks, and more bones. "We're getting close," the little knight continued expertly (although he had never actually seen a dragon in his life). "I'll soon be running my sword right through him."

"Will you?" cried Sir Gadabout, trying to give a little laugh but sounding more as if he were being throttled. "That's handy, because I think I left the kettle on at home, and I think I'd better—"

Suddenly, they heard a terrifying roar. Smoke was rising from behind a hill ahead of them.

"*My washing*!" Sir Gadabout screamed. "It looks like rain and I've left my socks out and—"

"*CHARGE*!" bellowed Sir Mistabit.

"*Wait*!" yelled Herbert. "We need a plan."

"We need some proper knights, more like," said a voice from inside his saddlebag.

They crept up the hill and peeped over. A dragon the size of a house was chasing a white goat that had a very peculiar way of running owing to having only one front leg and one back leg. Every now and then the dragon whooshed out a long fiery breath and each time the goat just managed to dart out of its way. But it was beginning to tire. It was only a matter of time before the dragon caught up with it.

"*Lucky*!" whispered Sir Mistabit.

"If you say so," murmured Sidney Smith.

"I think you and Sir Mistabit should attack him from different directions, Sire," Herbert

suggested. "That way, at least one of you might not get . . . er . . . slightly singed."

"We could try throwing stones at it from here," Sir Gadabout said hopefully. "Very *large* ones," he added, seeing the scornful looks on their faces. "Thrown very hard? Oh, all right then."

Sir Mistabit was already getting back on his

horse. "I'll charge from the east, you charge from the west!"

Within seconds the two knights were circling at high speed, preparing to attack.

But were they too late? The dragon had pounced on the exhausted goat and had her in its razor-sharp claws. The poor creature was bleating so pitifully even Sir Gadabout forgot his fear. He lowered his lance and charged.

Sir Mistabit did the same from the other side.

At first, the dragon didn't notice them. It was too busy lying with Lucky in its grasp, about to enjoy a good meal. But as the thunder of hooves grew louder, he looked up

sharply to see what was happening.

Just as the two knights were about to drive their lances into the huge beast, Sir Mistabit gave his war cry:"**BASH OR BUST**!"

He had a *very* loud voice for such a little man.

"You made me *jump*!" Sir Gadabout cried.

It wasn't a very bright thing to say.

Buck skidded to a halt just millimetres short of the dragon and gave an almighty kick with his back legs. Sir Gadabout sailed through the air and landed on top of the dragon's head.

The dragon leaped to its feet and Sir Mistabit hurtled on under its belly.

Sidney Smith sank back into Herbert's saddlebag with a groan and covered his head with his paws.

"*Heeeelp!*" screeched Sir Gadabout, clinging doggedly to the dragon's ears as it tried to flick him off.

"*Attack!*" bellowed Sir Mistabit, spurring on his horse. But the horse had already had its tail singed by the dragon's fiery breath and was not feeling quite as brave as its master. Instead of charging at the dragon, Sir Mistabit ended up galloping in circles around the creature, shouting and cursing.

The dragon had never seen anything quite like it. Something – he didn't know what – was on his head, making a weird high-pitched noise and pulling painfully on his ears; one horse was jumping up and down, kicking and whinnying, and another was speeding round and round him in circles.

The dragon became so dizzy trying to keep his eyes on everything that was going on that he toppled over and even lying on his back the world still seemed to be spinning very fast.

Sir Gadabout fell off and clattered to the ground.

"*Victory!*" Sir Mistabit cried. "No dragon can withstand the sharp point of my lance!" The small fact that the dragon had never felt the sharp point of his lance hardly seemed

worth quibbling over in the circumstances.

But had they been in time to save Lucky?

While the dragon was still rolling helplessly on its back, Sidney Smith felt brave enough to come out of Herbert's saddlebag. He crept closer to see what had become of the unfortunate mascot.

"Oh, *great*," he sighed, holding up what looked suspiciously like one of Lucky's two

remaining legs. "This is all that's left, thanks to our friends the nutty knights."

"No!" replied Herbert. "I saw Lucky escape!"

"On one leg?" Sidney Smith asked, raising his eyebrows and twitching his whiskers in disbelief.

"Yes!" Herbert insisted. "When the dragon fell over she got away – somehow."

"Then lead the way!" cried Sir Mistabit.

Sir Gadabout picked himself up very carefully and groggily. "Are you sure it's worth it?" he groaned. "After all, there's not much left to rescue."

"*We'll* be the ones who need rescuing before long," Sidney Smith said as he watched the dragon beginning to recover its senses. "Let's go!"

As soon as Herbert had calmed Buck down and Sir Gadabout could get back on him, they continued with their rescue mission. Surely Lucky couldn't have got far?

5

The Circus

They headed in the direction Herbert had seen Lucky take, thinking they must easily catch up with her. But very soon they came to a forest and it was impossible to tell which way to go. They searched for hours, without

success, and as darkness fell they had to set up camp for the night deep in the forest.

It was a troubled night. Sir Gadabout had never camped in a forest before, and he was rather worried by the hooting of owls, the howling of wolves, and the strange rustling noises of nocturnal creatures moving about. He dreamt that a dragon had thrown him into a frying pan with some bacon. "*I'm not a sausage!*" he whimpered repeatedly in his sleep, keeping everyone else awake.

Next day they travelled for miles without seeing a soul until late in the afternoon when they emerged from the forest and saw a farmhouse. A little old lady was throwing corn to the chickens in her yard.

"Let's ask her if she's seen Lucky," said Herbert.

"I'd never have thought of that," commented the sarcastic cat.

Sir Gadabout and Sir Mistabit approached the woman. She was small and frail with white hair and a kindly face.

"Good-day, madam," said Sir Gadabout. "I am a knight of—"

"Hello, young man!" the woman said. "You must be worn out. Come in and have a nice cup of tea."

"But we're looking for—"

"I know just how tiring it is when you have to take your children everywhere with you!"

Herbert and Sir Mistabit glowered at her.

"And *cats*!" she continued, spotting Sidney Smith and tweaking his ears rather too hard. "We know what naughty things *they* get up to in the flower beds!"

"I can assure you, madam," said Sidney Smith indignantly, "that I do not, and never have—"

"*Ooh*, I say – almost sounds human, doesn't he? There's a clever puss!" She tweaked his ears again and before they knew it she had marched them all into her farmhouse for a nice cup of tea. The last thing they wanted, while Lucky was still hopping away, was to stop for a nice cup of tea . . . followed by a nice piece of cake . . . followed by some nice home-made scones . . . But as it happened, it turned out to be worth it – *eventually*.

When they finally managed to explain about the goat, she said, "It just so happens I was looking after a stray goat with only one leg, poor thing. But then I found someone who could give her a good home."

"*WHERE*?" cried the four of them together and jumping to their feet.

"Eh? Oh, I think he runs some kind of circus in Lower Downham. *Loves* animals!"

"Thank you very much," Sir Gadabout said. And they hurried out before she could make them another nice cup of tea.

Lower Downham was about ten miles away

but just before getting to the village the would-be goat rescuers came upon a very large red-and-white striped tent. As they came closer they could see jugglers practising, clowns tripping over, and lion tamers taming – the exact kind of thing they had in circuses in Sir Gadabout's day.

"Looks like the circus," said Sir Gadabout.

"Oh? And there I was thinking it was a funeral procession . . ." Sidney Smith remarked.

Sir Mistabit dismounted and asked one of the clowns if he'd seen the goat.

"You'd better ask Signor Fettuccini the ringmaster."

As he was going to find Signor Fettuccini, the clown called back to Sir Mistabit. "Are you any good at falling off horses? We could do with a funny little chap like you in our act—"

"I'm *not* LITTLE!" snapped Sir Mistabit, straightening himself up as much as possible.

Sidney Smith sauntered over to the clown. "Forget it. You're out of your league, mate. We've got the best two clowns in the business here."

Signor Fettuccini was busy painting some kind of sign or poster. Herbert was detailed to talk to him. Neither he nor any of the others could speak Italian but at least Herbert owned an atlas.

"BONJOUR," shouted Herbert in a very loud voice, hoping it might help. "WE ARE LOOKING FOR A GOAT." He made a bleating noise that was supposed to sound like a goat but actually sounded more like a hungry guinea pig.

"THE GOAT IS A *WHITE* GOAT. SEE…" said Herbert, pulling out the elasticated waistband of his underpants – the only white thing he could find.

Signor Fettuccini was an elderly gentleman wearing a very impressive purple cloak and matching felt hat. As he watched Herbert making noises like a guinea pig and pulling at his underpants, his eyes began to swivel around wildly, as if looking for an escape route or possibly a big stick with which to defend himself.

"THE GOAT IS NOT ALL THERE."

Herbert lifted one of his legs in the air and kept patting it with the hand that wasn't holding his underpants. "NOT ONE AT EACH CORNER – *NO* – BUT ONLY ONE – SEE?"

Sidney Smith groaned. "Even I can't make him out, and I *know* what he's trying to say."

"I think it's rather good," said Sir Gadabout.

"You speak his language," the cat pointed out.

"What *is* he on about?" asked Signor Fettuccini in a decidedly English accent.

"We ... we thought you were Italian," mumbled Sir Gadabout.

"What for?"

"Never mind," interjected Sir Mistabit. "Have you seen a stray goat lately?"

"No, I haven't." They noticed him trying to cover up the sign he had been painting.

"Thank you, my man. We bid you good day," said Sir Gadabout.

But Sidney Smith had nipped under Signor Fettucini's legs to get a good look at the poster he had been painting. "It says *Guiseppe and his Amazing Hopping Goat!*" the cat declared.

"It isn't a *real* goat," laughed Signor Fettuccini. "It's a ... a poodle."

"With one leg?" asked Sidney Smith, studying the picture on the sign.

"Ooh, no – that's just my bad painting," the ringmaster assured him. "I'm not very good at legs, so I decided just to do the one."

At that moment, a man with an enormous belly sauntered along. "Got her to jump through a hoop, boss!" he cried excitedly. And hopping right behind him was Lucky!

"Get the goat!" roared Sir Mistabit.

Signor Fettuccini pushed Sir Mistabit over and ran. "Quick, Bill – don't let them get it!" The pair of them ran into the Big Top – the gigantic tent where the circus was held – with Sir Gadabout and the others in hot pursuit. They soon had the two men and the goat surrounded. Lucky, having finally noticed her long-lost master, was bleating to join him but was tightly held on a piece of rope.

"You might as well hand her over," Sir Mistabit said firmly. "You can't get away from us now."

"Oh, can't they?" growled a deep voice. Coming up behind them was the circus strongman, a gigantic, muscular fellow

covered in tattoos.

Sir Gadabout strode to meet him. "Now look here, I am a Knight of the Round Table—"

"Oh − *round*, is it?" The strongman picked Sir Gadabout up off the ground and proceeded to crumple him up in his armour like some people crush drinks cans. "Well, now *you're* round, too!" And he bowled Sir Gadabout at his comrades and knocked them over like skittles.

Sir Mistabit sprang to his feet and made a dash for Lucky. He was too nippy for the strongman but a flying figure suddenly sent him sprawling. A trapeze artist had leapt from one of the high swings and landed right on top of the miniature knight.

"*Retreat!*" Sir Gadabout cried dizzily from inside his ball of armour as it spun round and round on the sawdust floor.

Sir Mistabit had been pretty well squashed by the blow from above and was now only about half his previous height. It looked as though they had been defeated, and poor Lucky was bleating sadly.

But then, Signor Fettuccini pointed to one of the trapeze swings way up in the roof of

the Big Top. "What on earth is that?"

There was a shriek of "*BANZAI!*" and a turtle wearing a quite snazzy leotard launched itself like a guided missile.

CRACK! He caught the strongman on the head like a coconut at a fair.

BUMP, BANG, WHACK! He bounced from one head to another like a stone skimming across the water until all the baddies were lying on the ground groaning.

The turtle punched the air triumphantly.

"*YES!*"

"Dr McPherson!" cried Sidney Smith in admiration. "You finally got it right!"

(They later discovered that the rabbit Dr McPherson had been riding had a cousin in Lower Downham.)

When they arrived back at Camelot they caused quite a stir. Sir Mistabit was about the size of a milk carton and waddled along like an accordion on legs. Sir Gadabout was rolled home by Herbert, with Sidney Smith pestering him to see if Sir Gadabout would bounce.

But ever since the cat had kicked the ball of armour that was Sir Gadabout between two trees and shouted "*GOAL!*", Herbert had totally ignored him.

Sir Melville, in charge of the Knights of the Green Cross, was slightly disappointed that rather less of his goat had come back than had

set off, but he soon cheered up when Guinevere knocked up three very stylish wooden
legs for Lucky.

There was still the small matter of the
contest between Sir Mistabit and Sir Gadabout. It was a *very* close run thing. Everyone
knew deep down that Sir Gadabout was still

the Worst Knight in the World but they were
so thankful to get Lucky back it was quite a
while before they mentioned it again.

Sir Gadabout

and the Little Horror

for Heather and Philip

1

Castle Stonefist

A long, long time ago, well before anyone had won the top prize on *Who Wants to be a Millionaire?* there was a castle called Soggysocks. This was a very unusual name for a castle, but then it was a very unusual castle. The knights who lived there took in washing and ironing from villages far and wide, and generally very little else happened there. Some knights became so bored that they fell asleep standing up.

This would make an extremely dull story – but fortunately, not far from the castle called Soggysocks was another one called Camelot. This was a magnificent building whose stout walls kept out all invaders (except the knights of Soggysocks who came to collect Camelot's dirty clothes every fortnight).

The famous King Arthur lived in Camelot. He was a well-loved king and a powerful warrior, but he never had quite as much laundry as the other knights because he had dry skin and didn't sweat very much. Also, the T-shirts he wore on, say, Wednesday, he tended to wear again as a vest on Thursday. This didn't always go down well with his beautiful wife Guinevere, who would have preferred him to wear a clean T-shirt every day. However, she was so busy making ironing-boards for the knights of Soggysocks that she never had time to check on King Arthur's underwear.

But this story doesn't start at Camelot – nor even at Soggysocks, though the knights there had just received an exciting consignment of laundry from a famous celebrity. (I'm not allowed to say who, and anyway it was long before she married David Beckham.)

Where was I? Oh, yes: this story begins at the gates of Castle Stonefist, many days ride to the north of Camelot. Here waited Sir Percy, King Arthur's calmest, cleverest, most polite knight. He never lost his temper. And because of this King Arthur had chosen him for a special mission, which is why he was waiting at Castle Stonefist, where he would have to deal with Lord Stonefist, a powerful baron with a large army. Lord Stonefist had once been at war with King Arthur, and even came close to winning. Things had been rather tricky between them ever since, so Guinevere came up with the idea of allowing Lord Stonefist's young son to come to Camelot for extra-special training with the famous knights of the Round Table.

Sir Percy had the skills to ensure that nothing would go wrong during the talks with Lord Stonefist (who had a bit of a temper) and that his son would be safely delivered to Camelot. With Sir Percy was another

knight who did not have quite so many skills.
In fact some said he had no skills at all, and
most said he was the Worst Knight in the
World. This was, of course, Sir Gadabout,
who had been sent along because ... well,
King Arthur could think of nothing else to
do with him.

Sir Gadabout was wearing a brand-new
suit of armour which Guinevere had made
from wood left over from a new batch of
ironing-boards she had been working on.
(Those were cleverly made in the actual

shape of a shirt, so that you could iron it all
in one go and didn't have to fiddle about
with it and end up forgetting which sleeve
you had done.) Because it was a hot summer,
Guinevere had fastened the pieces of Sir
Gadabout's armour loosely together with
leather straps to let more air in. As Sir
Gadabout trotted along on his horse, the
pieces of wood jangled together and he
sounded rather like a wind-chime, which
kept everyone amused on the long journey
north. For a while.

With Sir Gadabout were his usual helpers. Herbert was his squire, or personal attendant. He was young, short and stocky and incredibly loyal to his master through thick and thin. Travelling inside Herbert's saddlebag was a rather overweight ginger cat called Sidney Smith. He wasn't incredibly loyal either to Sir Gadabout or Herbert. He knew what they were like, and just came along for a laugh.

But he was useful to them in one way, because Sidney Smith was no ordinary, overweight ginger moggy; he happened to be the cat of the great wizard Merlin. On this occasion Merlin had taught them a spell in case they got fed up with the long, slow journey and wanted to get it over with quickly. All they had to do was chant the magic words, and their horses would go ten times faster without getting tired!

Sir Gadabout had been very excited about the spell, and had been asking to use it ever since they had left Camelot. Even though his new horse, Buck, was much faster than his poor old one (though a lot more temperamental) the spell would give him the chance to ride faster than anyone had *ever* ridden! But Merlin had told them it could only be

used once, and as it was such lovely weather and there was no hurry, the others wanted to take their time (despite the wind-chimes). Sir Percy, who was in charge of the expedition, told Sir Gadabout he would have to wait till the return journey. But being the clever knight he was, he said it in such a way as to make Sir Gadabout think he was getting his own way. This was exactly why Sir Percy had been chosen to deal with Lord Stonefist, with his very short temper and very large army. Goodness knows what would happen if the meeting had been left in Sir Gadabout's hands …

So there they were, outside the gates of the castle, preparing to collect Lord Stonefist's son.

"Now, leave all the talking to me," said Sir Percy. "After all," he added, seeing Sir Gadabout's disappointed look, "we have to keep up your reputation as the strong, silent type!"

"What about his reputation as the biggest bungler in armour?" queried Sidney Smith. Herbert pressed the cat's head into the saddlebag and fastened the strap.

"*Strong silent type!*" Sir Gadabout repeated proudly to himself. "Very well. But can I say the 'Ten Times Faster' spell when we go home?"

"Certainly," said Sir Percy.

Sir Gadabout and Herbert dismounted and took a drink from their flasks. Hearing the trickling water, Sidney Smith managed to squeeze out of the saddlebag and join them.

"Oh dear ..." exclaimed Sir Gadabout suddenly. "I think I've forgotten the spell!"

Herbert scratched his head. "I think it starts: *Horse so strong* ..."

"That's it!" agreed Sir Gadabout. "*Horse so strong, I am your master* ..."

"I really don't think you should carry on!" warned Sidney Smith.

But Sir Gadabout was too excited to listen. "*Hear these words and go TEN TIMES FASTER!*"

"WHOAAAAAAAH!!!" shrieked Sir Percy.

If his horse had been fired from a cannon it could hardly have taken off more violently.

His cry faded as he disappeared in a blur over a distant hill. All that could be seen was a trail of dust where he had been.

"Whoops," said Sir Gadabout.

"He sounded a bit upset, sire," commented Herbert.

"With a touch of panic thrown in," added Sidney Smith.

"Funny," said Sir Gadabout. "He always seemed such a calm fellow ... "

They all stood looking at the long trail of dust as it settled gradually into the shimmering earth. Then they turned to look at the formidable walls of Castle Stonefist. Then they looked back at the horizon.

"He'll probably be back in a minute," said Sir Gadabout hopefully.

2

Later

"He'll probably be back in a day or two," said Sir Gadabout as they woke, stretching and yawning next day …

3

Much Later

"I don't think he's coming back," said Sir Gadabout at the end of the week ...

4

Later Still

"We're kippered," grumbled Sidney Smith, surveying the Sir Percyless horizon.

"It looks like someone else will have to deal with the terrible and powerful Lord Stonefist," Sir Gadabout admitted. "Er, why is everyone looking at me?"

In fact, Sir Percy's horse had neither stopped nor slowed down till reaching Camelot, hundreds of miles away. All Sir Percy's fillings had dropped out, and he had to have a very powerful ointment applied to his bottom three times a day for the next six weeks.

"I heard that Lord Stonefist once turned a man completely inside out with his bare hands just for coughing too loudly," fibbed Sidney Smith mischievously.

Sir Gadabout coughed. He couldn't help

himself. And then he began to shake so much that his wooden armour played what sounded like a snappy Irish jig.

"I also heard," said the cat with a mean chuckle, "that he once declared war on Prussia because someone put one sugar in his tea instead of two. And he wasn't even a Prussian!"

Sir Gadabout gulped.

"I don't believe a word of it!" cried Herbert. Funnily enough this last tale was true, although Sidney Smith wasn't to know that.

"And he *hates* wind chimes!" continued Sidney Smith, enjoying himself.

Sir Gadabout made a whimpering noise like a hungry guinea-pig.

And so the three of them nervously approached the dark, gigantic gates of Castle Stonefist. Herbert and Sidney Smith secretly feared for what might happen if by some strange chance Sir Gadabout should upset Lord Stonefist. Well, actually Herbert feared this secretly. Sidney Smith declared, "The fool's going to start a *war*. That's a first even for us."

Sir Gadabout himself was walking in a

strangely slow and stiff manner, trying not to sound like a wind-chime. And he could be heard muttering, "*Two sugars not one ... Two sugars not one ...*"

5

Little Roger

Later that day, Sir Gadabout, Herbert and Sidney Smith found themselves in a large room inside Castle Stonefist. Lord Stonefist had been keeping them waiting for two hours already. The rumour was that one of his knights had burped during breakfast, and the baron was at that moment dangling the unfortunate culprit over the castle battlements by the ankles and lecturing him about unpleasant noises at the breakfast table. On hearing this, Sir Gadabout took to standing rigidly like a statue, even more terrified of the wind-chime sounds his armour made.

Just when they were beginning to get extremely bored, the door opened and a small boy struggled in dragging a large wooden, jewel-encrusted chest. Once the chest was inside the room, the boy closed the door and

looked at them all solemnly. He had big, honest-looking blue eyes, neatly combed hair and was smartly dressed.

"I am Roger, Lord Stonefist's squire. I'm sorry to have to tell you that my master has run away with the Queen of Gargantua and won't be coming back ever, so you might as well all go home. But before he went he asked me to divide some of his riches between you to make up for your wasted journey."

He opened the lid of the chest, and his face was lit up by the sun reflecting off the many wonderful treasures inside. "Take whatever you want," added Roger, "but be quick and then leave immediately. The, er, Inspector of Castles says the walls are in a bad condition and liable to fall down at any moment."

And with that, he disappeared. Sir Gadabout and the others were shocked at this news — but the precious goods in the chest managed to take their minds off it. Herbert was soon wearing a tunic that was far too big for him, made of the finest silk embroidered with gold, and he had various pieces of priceless jewellery to take home to his mum (or so he claimed). Sidney Smith had a feeling there was something fishy about the boy's story — but he wasn't complaining as he had found a solid silver dish with diamonds around the rim. He thought it would make a marvellous Sunday-best milk dish.

Sir Gadabout, meanwhile, was brandishing a magnificent sword which had jewels in the hilt and diamonds set along the gleaming, razor-sharp blade. It was almost as impressive as King Arthur's famous Excalibur. *And* there was a matching shield.

"We'd better go now, sire," said Herbert at last, glancing nervously at the walls around them.

At first, Sir Gadabout was in no hurry. By now, he was in the middle of a fight with an imaginary enemy (but not doing very well – Sir Gadabout even lost imaginary fights). But a deep, heavy rumbling sound made them all stop and look around. It sounded like the walls were coming down already.

"Quick! Head for the hills!" cried Sir Gadabout in a panic.

The heavy rumbling was in fact nothing to do with the castle walls (which were as strong and firm as could be) but was the sound of Lord Stonefist approaching very quickly, and in a *very* bad mood (he was always in a bad mood, but when he was in a *very* bad mood you had to look out).

The door burst open, and there stood a tall figure with a broad chest and muscular arms. And that was only Lord Stonefist's little brother Ernie. When the baron himself came in, he was even bigger. He was dressed all in black, with a great cloak that swirled about him like the wings of a gigantic bird of prey, and black gauntlets with sharp silver studs sticking out of them. (He found these useful for punching holes in paper; that way he didn't have to use one of those little machines that always get jammed.)

Lord Stonefist stood in the doorway, blocking out the light and casting a shadow over the three visitors. He slowly raised a hand and pointed a studded finger right at Sir Gadabout.

"He's got me sword! Me precious *Lightning Strike!*" gasped Lord Stonefist. He had a curiously high-pitched voice that sounded as though it was on the verge of tears.

"No wonder he's heading for the hills," muttered Ernie.

Sir Gadabout tried to explain, but no sensible words would come out (not that they often did). "N-n-n-not stealing … walls … Queen of Gargantua … wind-chimes crumbling …" He was trembling so much that his armour sounded more like a machine-gun than wind-chimes, and splinters flew around the room so that everyone had to keep ducking.

Lord Stonefist's pointing finger moved to Herbert. "Me best tunic! Me wife's finest jewels!"

"Hanging's too good for 'em," Ernie whined.

"Find a cat! Any cat! Chop its tail and ears

off!" wailed the baron.

"That'll make you feel better," Ernie whispered soothingly. "For a start!"

"Yes, sire," said a guard standing beside Lord Stonefist. But before he could do anything, Ernie had spotted Sidney Smith.

"Cat! He'll do!"

The guard advanced on Sidney Smith, drawing a sharp knife from his belt.

"Now, look here my good man," said the cat in a stern voice he had picked up from Merlin. The guard was so surprised to hear a ginger cat talking that he did stop.

"This is all a misunderstanding," Sidney Smith explained. "We were told that you had run away with the Queen of Gargantua ..."

"WHAT?!" cried Lord Stonefist.

"Such lies," hissed Ernie into his brother's ear. "Such a virtuous lady!"

"And," continued Sidney Smith, "that we could take what we wanted if we left quickly because the castle is about to fall down. So there!"

"FALL DOWN?!" shrieked Lord Stonefist.

"Vile insult," murmured Ernie. "Finest castle in the north."

Lord Stonefist took a step closer to them.

So did Ernie. "Before I kill you all slowly and painfully, pray tell me – WHY?" His squeaky, high voice started to sound weepy. "*Why spoil my day?*" His eyes began to water. "Why ruin my life?" His bottom lip began to tremble. "Why steal my –" and then it all became too much for him, and he turned his back on them and began to blub like a baby. "*I'm not crying!*" he sobbed, his cloak wrapped round his head.

"Not crying," added Ernie. "Fly in his eye – you all saw it. Lord Stonefist *never* cries, never mind what anyone might tell you."

"It was HIM!" shouted Herbert suddenly. He had just noticed Roger lurking in the doorway. "He told us all the lies!"

"*I never!*" replied Roger sweetly and innocently.

"You little horror!" Sidney Smith accused.

"*Now they accuse my only son!*" wailed Lord Stonefist into his cloak.

"But that's your squire," said Sir Gadabout.

Ernie shook his head. "His only son. A sweet son. A perfect, well-mannered son. Little horror indeed."

"*Cut things off them!*" blubbed Lord Stonefist. "*Stick things into them — long, sharp things.*"

"I've had enough of this," Sidney Smith declared. He had just remembered a spell he'd seen Merlin perform. "*Forget my name ...*" he began chanting.

"Eh?" said Lord Stonefist.

"*Forget my face ...*"

"What?" queried Ernie.

"*Forget we met, and begin again!*"

"Umm — who are these people?" Lord Stonefist asked.

Sidney Smith finished the spell:

"Dry those tears,
Downcast chappie,
Lose that frown
And BE HAPPY!"

An amazing change came over Lord Stonefist. The spell was so powerful that his tears dried up and his face brightened as if lit by a sunbeam. He began to giggle like a little boy being tickled. "Ah!" he chortled. "You must be the visitors from Camelot. Look after young Roger for us, won't you. Though you won't have any trouble – he's a little angel!"

"A little cherub!" tittered Ernie.

Sir Gadabout froze on the spot as Lord Stonefist pinched one of his cheeks and Ernie teasingly kissed him on the other. "Er ... c-can someone explain ..." he stammered.

"Later. *The spell soon wears off*," said Sidney Smith, trying to hurry their exit from Castle Stonefist with sweet little Roger.

"Have a safe journey!" Lord Stonefist called as they departed.

"A pleasant one!" added Ernie brightly.

Still Sir Gadabout hesitated, scratching his helmet and trying to figure things out.

"*GO!*" cried Sidney Smith. "The spell is wearing off!"

Lord Stonefist suddenly gave his head a shake and rubbed his eyes. He saw before him the people he had caught stealing his sword and valuables. A dark expression came over his face. "And tell King Arthur ... tell him ... THIS MEANS *WAR!*" he whined, and promptly burst into tears.

"And Lord Stonefist's been peeling an onion, so don't start any rumours!" shouted Ernie as Sir Gadabout and Co. galloped away.

6

The Joke Turns Sour

"Now, my boy," said Sir Gadabout as they began the long ride south. "What kind of things do you like to do?"

Roger smiled sweetly at Sir Gadabout. "Flower arranging, sir, and helping people, and skipping!"

"Skipping the truth, more like," remarked Sidney Smith, who had recognised the little horror for what he was.

"Please keep that horrid cat away from me, sir," Roger pleaded. "I'm afraid I might catch fleas!"

Sidney Smith growled like a Staffordshire bull terrier.

It was another hot day, and when they reached a river of cool, sparkling water, they stopped for a drink. Not long after setting off again, Sir Gadabout was heard to say,

"Goodness me – the world is turning upside down!"

When they looked at him, his saddle was gradually slipping down Buck's side, and Sir Gadabout was going with it. Finally, he was hanging upside down.

"Something is definitely not right here," he commented as his head bumped along the ground.

They discovered that his saddle had been deliberately loosened during their stop by the river.

"It was him!" accused Roger, pointing at Sidney Smith.

Although Sidney denied it, he *had* played tricks on them in the past, and Sir Gadabout gave him a suspicious look before they set off again.

They had arranged to spend the night at the castle of a friend of King Arthur's – Sir Pelligrew the Portly – and they arrived there just as it was beginning to grow dark.

"Welcome, welcome!" chuckled Sir Pelligrew the Portly, who was, well, *portly*. "I want to have the grass in my garden washed – do you know where I should take it?"

Sir Gadabout was perplexed by this question. "I, er, I'm not quite sure."

"Why, I think I shall take it to the laundry! *Lawn-dree* — get it?"

Herbert laughed so much that he was rolling on the floor kicking his legs in the air. Only Sir Pelligrew himself, whose laugh seemed to echo around inside his huge belly then erupt into the air like a hurricane, laughed louder. Sidney Smith sniffed (which you will find is a bit of a tongue-twister if you try to say it quickly) and said he'd seen better jokes on ice-lolly sticks.

Sir Gadabout simply didn't get it. "But if you take your grass to the laundry, won't all the bits get stuck inside the machine …"

This made Sir Pelligrew laugh even louder, and all the candles in the hall they had entered blew out, and servants had to come rushing in to light them again (it seemed as though they had had plenty of practice at this).

"King Arthur is a very, very good friend of mine, and I'm putting you in my finest guest rooms," said Sir Pelligrew once he had got his breath back from all the laughing. He and King Arthur had become very good friends ever since the king had actually laughed his socks off at one of Sir Pelligrew's corniest jokes.

Sir Pelligrew the Portly took them along a corridor until they came to the third door on the left, which he threw open. When Sir Gadabout, Herbert and Sidney Smith went inside they found it was a lovely, cosy room, with comfortable beds and beautiful decorations. No one noticed that Roger was still hanging around suspiciously outside.

"Now," said Sir Pelligrew, "you will make sure you have a pencil with you, won't you."

"A pencil?" repeated Sir Gadabout.

"Well," chortled Sir Pelligrew, "you'll need

something to *draw* the curtains with, won't you?!" Unfortunately he laughed so much that he blew the curtains down. However, a team of servants scurried in immediately and replaced them, just as if they were used to doing it all the time.

Herbert laughed until he cried. Sir Gadabout couldn't figure it out, since the servants had just drawn the curtains ... Sidney Smith groaned, "Close the door, quick – I can't stand many more jokes like this."

"Ah! A little pussy!" exclaimed Sir

Pelligrew, noticing Sidney Smith for the first time.

Sidney Smith's tail waved in the air and the fur bristled on his back – he hated being called that.

Sir Pelligrew pretended to whisper something to Sir Gadabout, though he was saying it loud enough for them all to hear. "I never trust cats with anything important myself ..."

"And why not?" Sidney Smith demanded.

"Because they always get in a FLAP!"

Sidney Smith didn't reply, he simply slammed the door in Sir Pelligrew the Portly's face – but his laughter blew it wide open again, making him roar like an elephant being tickled.

"I wouldn't say cats get in a flap especially," mused Sir Gadabout, looking very puzzled. "Sometimes dogs get a bit excited, but – "

"What's the difference," interrupted Sidney Smith irritably, "between an astronaut and Sir Gadabout?"

"I don't know," Herbert replied.

"One's got his head in space, the other's got lots of space in his head."

"Er, which one's which?" Sir Gadabout asked.

Roger met Sir Pelligrew the Portly outside. He had a plan. He lived a very lazy, spoiled life at Castle Stonefist, and had no desire to go through all the years of hard work involved in becoming a knight of the Round Table. It would be bad enough having to do all the training – but the thought of being taught by *Sir Gadabout* of all people meant that he would stoop to anything to get out of it.

"My father didn't really send me with these people," Roger claimed, making tears come into his big blue eyes as he looked imploringly at Sir Pelligrew.

"Really?"

"Oh, no. They've kidnapped me and are

going to sell me into slavery. But don't tell them I told you – Sir Gadabout said he would chop me up and feed me to his hamster if I said anything."

"Well, I never! Knights of the Round Table don't usually act like that. I'll have to think about it – I'll talk to you again in the morning. Good night, young fellow, and keep safe!"

Roger gave Sir Pelligrew a goodnight kiss on the cheek. "You remind me of my favourite uncle," he said sweetly. "Good night!"

However, a different Roger rejoined the others – the Little Horror. He assumed a very shocked expression. "I've just got a secret message from one of the servants – Sir Pelligrew plans to kidnap me!"

"Whatever for?" asked Sir Gadabout.

"Well, er, he hasn't got any children of his own, and he's afraid that when he dies there will be nobody left to go on telling all the jokes he's thought up. He's going to keep me locked in a little dark room until I've learned them all!"

"There could be no worse form of torture," Sidney Smith gasped. "But it serves you right."

Herbert didn't agree. "I'll take Roger's place," he volunteered heroically.

"No!" said Sir Gadabout. "We shall be on our guard, and slip away at first light!"

While they were asleep that night the Little Horror was busy creeping around the castle. Very early the next day, they were woken by a big commotion coming from the vicinity of Sir Pelligrew's bedroom.

Sir Pelligrew the Portly was fast asleep, snoring very loudly. When he breathed in, his large belly rose in the air like a whale leaping out of the water. When he breathed out, a feather on his face was blown three feet into the air, then floated back down again. Beside the bed was a sign:

COME AND SEE THE
FAT FOOLE SNORE!!
10p TODAY ONLY
CURTESY OF GADABOUT ENTERPRISES
(THIS MAN IS SO DAFT HE DOESN'T
REELIZE WE ARE KIDNAPPING AN
INNACENT LITTLE BOY)

A crowd had followed a series of similar signs from the castle gates, and were now standing around Sir Pelligrew's bed laughing and cheering at the sight before them.

At first, Sir Pelligrew dreamt that people were laughing at his jokes. But eventually the noise woke him up. He spat the feather out – and read the sign.

"So it's true! Sir Gadabout is going to kidnap Roger," he bellowed. "I must save the boy!"

Meanwhile, Sir Gadabout and Co. were hurriedly getting dressed when they heard Sir Pelligrew charging along the corridors shouting, "GET THE BOY! GET THE BOY BEFORE THEY ESCAPE!" (Fortunately for Sir Gadabout, all Sir Pelligrew's guards and servants, instead of joining the chase, were dutifully laughing and

congratulating their lord on his latest joke.)

"So it's true!" cried Sir Gadabout.

"Quick – through the window!" said Herbert.

Roger had returned to Sir Gadabout's room so that Sir Pelligrew would believe he was being kidnapped. He planned to nip into a wardrobe while they were escaping – but his pockets were now so full of the ten-pence pieces he had collected from spectators that they slowed him down. Sidney Smith, who had been keeping a close eye on him, tripped him up as he tried to put his plan into action. Herbert, thinking he had stumbled, scooped him up with his big fist and lifted him through the window.

As they galloped away, they heard Sir Pelligrew shouting, "THIS IS NO JOKE! KIDNAP! MURDER! WAR ON SIR GADABOUT AND CAMELOT!"

Sidney Smith's head came out of Herbert's saddlebag once they were in the clear. "I reckon the kid had something to do with this," he hissed.

"*I never*!" cried Roger, opening his big blue eyes wide and fluttering his eyelashes.

"Roger saved the day!" Sir Gadabout agreed. "If he hadn't told us about Sir Pelligrew's treachery, he would have been taken from us!"

Roger looked at Sidney Smith and grinned. The cat narrowed his eyes and gave him his most hateful look, then disappeared back into the saddlebag muttering horrible things.

7

The Left Against the Right

Sir Pelligrew the Portly was hardly the fastest rider in the world, and even Sir Gadabout and his companions soon managed to leave him well behind. The next few days' riding were fairly uneventful. The nights were so warm they were able to sleep out under the stars. But when dark clouds began to approach rapidly on a strong breeze, and they saw distant flashes of lightning, they decided to find shelter for the night.

They came to a crossroads with a signpost in the middle which said, *Castle Left – Right*.

"I think we ought to see if we can shelter there for the night," said Herbert, keeping an eye on the approaching thunderstorm. "But I'm not sure which way we're supposed to go . . ."

Sidney Smith's head popped up and sur-

veyed the scene. "Well I think it means 'Castle Left is to the right.' We go right."

"No, no," said Roger. "I know this area. It means 'Castle on the left – Castle Right'."

"Oh dear," said Sir Gadabout, completely flummoxed (which wasn't difficult for him). "Perhaps we should go straight on."

"Nonsensical nincompoop," muttered Sidney Smith.

Sir Gadabout, by the way, was no longer sounding like a wind-chime. He had found some sticky tape in Herbert's saddlebag and stuck hundreds of little bits all over his wooden armour to prevent the different pieces from jangling together.

"Sir," said Roger, gazing at Sir Gadabout with his honest blue eyes. "The left-hand road definitely leads to Castle Right, where we are bound to find a room for the night. You are one of my favourite knights in the whole world – I have always followed your adventures, and I would never lie to you."

"*Hmmph!*" snorted Sidney Smith.

Sir Gadabout proudly stuck his chest out so much that some of the bits of sticky tape burst open. "Roger is a very clever little boy, and I believe him. We turn left!"

The left-hand road took them as far as Happy Harry's House of Hats and then came to a dead-end. Herbert did buy himself a natty bearskin – one of those big black hats that soldiers wear outside Buckingham Palace – which he thought made him look taller. But that didn't get them any closer to the castle.

"I said we should have gone right for Castle Left, sir," Roger said sadly to Sir Gadabout.

"You said left to Castle Right!" accused Sidney Smith.

"*I never*! I do believe, little pussycat, that Sir Gadabout, who has one of the most brilliant minds and memories of all the knights of the Round Table, will recall that I said 'Right for Castle Left'."

Some more bits of sticky tape popped apart on Sir Gadabout's armour. "I remember it quite clearly. If only you'd listened to him we wouldn't have wasted all this time!"

Sidney Smith was so angry – not only that they wouldn't believe him, but especially at being called a "little pussycat" – that he almost exploded there and then. He sank back inside the saddlebag and sulked for quite some time.

They found Castle Left – for that was its name on account of the fact that they only employed left-handed knights, for some reason that has long ago been forgotten – just as the first big drops of rain began to splatter around them, and the thunder and lightning grew closer and louder. Unfortunately, Sir

Gadabout was extremely afraid of thunder and lightning. Every time he heard thunder, not only did it make him jump, but he invariably also waved his arms in the air and cried out for his mother in a spookily screeching voice.

The guards at Castle Left took them to the room of the owner, Sir Sinistral, whose room was the third door on the left (*all* the doors in this castle were on the left). Sir Gadabout explained who they were and why they were there – in a roundabout sort of way.

"I would normally let you stay for as long as you like," said Sir Sinistral, with a worried expression. "But you have come at a difficult time. Tomorrow we are going to be attacked by the army of the treacherous Sir Dexter. The reasons are long and complicated, but needless to say this will not be a safe place to remain."

"But Sir Gadabout is one of the greatest knights in the world," said Roger. "With him you are sure to win!"

"I was going to say that," said a rather disgruntled Herbert.

"Er ... one of the *greatest* knights? But I'd heard that he was ..."

"Well, you heard wrong!" interrupted Herbert. "He *is* one of the greatest knights."

"Except Sir Lancelot," added Sidney Smith. "And Sir Bors, and Sir Gawain, and —" Sidney Smith would have gone on to reel off the names of every knight he knew had he not been stopped by Herbert shoving one of his smelly socks into the cat's mouth.

But Sir Sinistral was desperate enough for *any* help, and agreed to let them stay.

As he took them to their room, Sir Gadabout was already becoming nervous

about the battle the next day. The rain had loosened the sticky tape on his armour, allowing the pieces to jangle again. His trembling seemed to be causing it to play a tune by one of those girl bands – whose name I can't quite remember. Not only that, but the loose bits of tape flapped and whistled around, providing a ghostly harmony.

"Er, interesting armour you Round Table knights have," commented Sir Sinistral as he bade them goodnight.

Next morning Sir Gadabout and Co. accompanied Sir Sinistral to the battlefield, where they were confronted by Sir Dexter and his powerful army. Black clouds hovered overhead, and thunder and lightning filled the air. Sir Sinistral's knights lined up on the

left, Sir Dexter's on the right. When Sir Gadabout saw the enemy, he insisted that he had forgotten to fold his pyjamas neatly before he had left, and was prevented from returning only after a desperate struggle.

Then a surprising thing happened. Sir Dexter himself rode forward alone and demanded to speak to them.

"I have heard that you have a knight of the Round Table with you – I think you must be getting desperate, Sir Sinistral."

"You'll never know how right you are," muttered Sidney Smith.

"Therefore," continued Sir Dexter, "I have

a suggestion. We are two powerful armies and a lot of blood will be shed today, whoever wins. So let us settle it by single combat. I challenge your famous knight to a duel to the death, the winner wins the war. Let ours be the only blood that is shed!"

"Sir Gadabout accepts the challenge!" Roger piped up at the top of his voice.

"*I was going to say that!*" complained Herbert. "Will you please stop doing that?"

At that moment lightning streaked through the dark sky and hit a tree, which burst into flames. At the same time, thunder made the ground shake beneath them.

Sir Gadabout's arms shot into the air like someone being held up at gunpoint. "*Mothuuuurgh!*" he screeched wildly, causing all the horses within earshot to buck and whinny frantically.

"Who or what is that?" asked Sir Dexter.

"Sir Gadabout of Camelot!" cried Herbert proudly, beating Roger to it.

Sir Dexter rode away with such a dark and evil laugh that the remaining sticky tape peeled off Sir Gadabout's armour and floated to the ground. The two knights prepared for battle.

8

The Forest of the Undead

When Sir Dexter's army saw Sir Gadabout, in his clinking-clanking armour, clumsily preparing to charge, they laughed out loud. Their own lord was bigger, stronger, and carrying the scars of many battles.

What nobody noticed was little Roger slipping away from Sir Sinistral's side and tiptoeing towards Sir Dexter's army. Nobody noticed, that is, except Sidney Smith. His sharp eyes didn't miss much, and he crept after the boy. The cat watched as Roger approached Sir Dexter's squire, and he leaned close to listen as the boy whispered something in the squire's ear.

Just as Sir Gadabout levelled his long spear and began to charge, the squire passed the whisper on to his master, and Sir Dexter suddenly turned very pale.

There was a gasp from Sir Dexter's army

as, instead of meeting Sir Gadabout head-on and knocking him into the middle of next week, Sir Dexter turned in panic and tried to escape!

Even Sir Sinistral seemed surprised, but Herbert said, "Great knights of the Round Table have this effect on the enemy, sire."

This was all especially strange as Sir Gadabout, who had long believed that the sharp points on spears were very dangerous, had covered the end of his with a large rubber ball. What only Sidney Smith knew was

that Roger had informed the squire that the thing on the end of Sir Gadabout's spear was actually a bomb!

Things began to go downhill fast.

Word in Sir Dexter's camp soon got round that they had been tricked by Sir Gadabout and his secret weapon. Sir Gadabout, who had been feeling very much the part, if somewhat surprised, as he chased the mighty Sir Dexter all over the place, suddenly saw the whole of the enemy army begin to surge towards him, crying "*TREACHERY!*"

"Er ... one at a time, good knights," Sir Gadabout protested feebly.

Then, an eagle-eyed knight on Sir Sinistral's side noticed Roger standing in Sir Dexter's camp, chuckling at the mayhem he had caused. "THE BOY'S A SPY! IT'S A TRICK!"

The upshot of all this was that Sir Gadabout, Herbert, Sidney Smith and Roger found themselves being pursued through three counties by two powerful armies of angry knights.

"It's not fair!" cried Sir Gadabout as he held on to Buck's reins for dear life. "I was winning!"

"Only because the brat said you had a bomb on the end of your spear," shouted Sidney Smith above the sound of galloping hooves.

"I never!" protested Roger.

He blinked his big blue eyes at Sir Gadabout. This time, Sir Gadabout looked at him, and wondered ...

Fortunately, large armies can't travel fast for long, and they were eventually left behind. *Unfortunately,* Sir Gadabout, in a moment of weakness, once more insisted that they took the Little Horror's advice on the way to go. The path they took led to a vast forest. There was a sign by the side of the path where it led into the trees:

"Ooeer!" remarked Herbert. Sidney Smith was, unusually for him, speechless. Even Roger looked a little pale. As for Sir Gadabout, he had lost so many pieces of wood from his armour during the headlong flight from the two armies that he was down to his Butterflies of the World underwear. It was not a pretty sight, and on seeing this sign he was shaking so much that the vibrations were travelling down his horse's body and causing the poor thing's horseshoes to come loose. "W-we'd better go round it," he stuttered.

But the forest stretched from one side to the other as far as the eye could see, and there seemed to be no choice but to enter.

It was another hot, sunny day – but inside the Forest of the Undead it was cool, dark and gloomy. The singing of the birds suddenly ceased, and Sir Gadabout and the rest of them felt as though a thousand pairs of eyes were watching their every step. The path twisted and turned until they had no idea where they were or which direction they were going in. The branches on either side seemed to be grabbing at them, trying to stop them from going further – or preventing them from getting away. The wind whispering in the leaves sounded like ghostly voices warning them to escape, if they still could. It was such a spooky place that they kept expecting something to jump out at them round every corner – but nothing did.

"Not so bad, after all," commented Sir Gadabout bravely from inside his own saddlebag, into which he had miraculously managed to squeeze his thin body.

But then night began to fall. Dark shapes and shadows could be seen moving here and there. Strange rustling sounds could be heard above and around them. Whenever they saw something moving, they called out: but no answer ever came.

When it had become almost completely dark, and they could barely make out the path before them, a huge, menacing figure suddenly loomed ahead of them, blocking their way.

"Who goes there?" challenged Sir Gadabout, his teeth chattering like castanets.

The reply was a laugh so evil it virtually made Sir Gadabout's Butterflies of the World underwear unravel. The foul breath from the laugh blew the leaves from the trees, as it echoed and thundered in the stillness of the night.

"*Mothuuuuuurgh!*" cried Sir Gadabout waving his arms out of the top of his saddlebag.

"*I am the Lord of the Undead,*" said the figure. "*Welcome to my realm!*"

9

The Three Deadly Challenges

"You are mine forever!" laughed the Lord of the Undead in his deep, echoey voice. His armour was black, and stained with the marks of an unimaginable passage of time. Where his face should have been inside his helmet was also blackness – except for two red eyes that burned like tiny flames. "While you live, you are surrounded by my knights – the Host of the Undead. And when the time comes for you to die, you will not die, but become Undead like the rest of us and haunt this place for all eternity!"

"I don't like the sound of that very much," Herbert remarked.

"Has he gone, yet?" squeaked a voice from inside Sir Gadabout's saddlebag.

"And because you have dared to enter my domain," continued the terrible figure, "you

must complete the Three Deadly Challenges …"

"Or what?" Sidney Smith challenged him.

The Lord of the Undead turned his piercing eyes on Sidney Smith. "Do you realise who you are talking to, pathetic creature?"

"Well, I didn't think it was my Aunty Gladys. We aren't doing your stupid challenges."

"Then you will die!"

"But you said we would become Undead – so how can you kill us?"

"Because … Look, will you stop asking awkward questions? People normally just go along with what I say – I'm highly terrifying, you know!"

"You look like an overgrown scarecrow to me, mate. The way I see it, we're doomed anyway – so we aren't doing even *one* Deadly Challenge!"

"Oh, *please*! It's so boring, living in here forever. This is the only fun I have!"

"No."

"*Pretty please!*"

"No!"

"Look, I'll make the Three Deadly Challenges easier. Much easier."

"Such as?"

"Find me ... oh, something green, something pretty, and a wild animal of some kind."

Sidney Smith thought for a moment. "Okay – you close your eyes and count to a hundred, and we'll go and do it."

"Now wait a minute ..." began the Lord of the Undead.

"I bet you can't count to a hundred!" Sidney Smith chided him.

"I jolly well can! I can count to a *thousand*!"

"Well, do it then."

"I will too!"

And with that, the Lord of the Undead closed his eyes and began to count.

"*Let's go, boys!*" whispered Sidney Smith urgently.

They all hurried past the fiend and soon left him far behind.

"Stop!" yelled Sir Gadabout after a few minutes.

"What?" Sidney Smith exclaimed.

"Just there – I saw something pretty!"

"We're not actually *doing* the challenge, sire," Herbert explained.

"But he'll be very disappointed …"

"As long as we stop messing about, we won't be around when he finds out," said

Sidney Smith. "Quick – he must be up to around six hundred already!"

They raced along the forest path as fast as they could in the darkness, stumbling on the uneven ground, branches lashing their faces. It wasn't long before they heard much terrible wailing and gnashing of teeth behind them: the Lord of the Undead and his many minions were in pursuit, thirsting for revenge at having been tricked.

For a while, no matter how fast they went they could hear the dreadful wailing and gnashing getting ever closer. But eventually Sir Gadabout's own pitiful wailing drowned everything else out, and they couldn't tell how quickly the Lord of the Undead was gaining on them.

Soon, they didn't have to listen for their pursuers – a glance over their shoulders revealed hundreds of ghostly figures rushing towards them.

"Keep going," cried Sidney Smith, who had by far the sharpest eyes. "I can see the edge of the forest!"

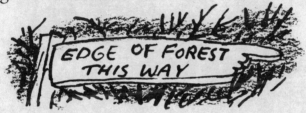

Now, Sir Gadabout stopped wailing, and like a prayer began to repeat, "*They can't come out of the forest … they can't come out of the forest …*" over and over again.

At long last they burst from the canopy of trees into open fields. Sir Gadabout looked back.

"*They're coming out of the forest!*
AAAAAAAAAARGH!"

Not even the Undead had heard a scream like the one emitted by Sir Gadabout, and the whole horde came to an awestruck halt, wondering what manner of strange creature

they were actually chasing. This allowed Sir Gadabout and Co. to escape at last.

Once it seemed they were clear of danger, at least for the time being, they all turned to little Roger.

"This was all your doing – *again*!" Herbert accused.

"I never!"

"I shall tell King Arthur, who will tell your father," added Sir Gadabout.

Seeing that he was on very thin ice, Roger showed his true colours. "A lot of good that will do!" he said, laughing at them all. "My father will believe *me*. Everyone always believes me – and I'll tell them it was all *your* fault!" And he ended with a laugh that sounded even nastier than that of the Lord of the Undead.

Worse still, Sir Gadabout had a horrible feeling that Roger was probably right. If he could make a great knight like himself believe his stories, what chance did anyone else stand? "We're all doomed! Finished!" he moaned.

"Worry not, Sir Madabout," whispered Sidney Smith, hopping into Sir Gadabout's lap. "I've got a plan ..."

10

King Alf and Queen Pete

On the morning that they came in sight of Camelot at long last, Sidney Smith rose very early while the rest of them were asleep, and hurried the last few miles to the castle on his own, unnoticed by any of the others ...

By the time Sir Gadabout, Herbert and Roger arrived at Camelot, the main gates were wide open, and two figures were there waiting to greet them. They were actually Alf, the castle caretaker, and Pete, his assistant. But Alf was wearing his poshest clothes and a crown made out of tin painted gold. Pete was wearing a dress and a wig of long blonde hair.

Sidney Smith strode forward. "Pray bow before their majesties, King Arthur and Queen Guinevere!" he commanded.

"But that's —"

Just before Sir Gadabout could give the

game away, Herbert did something he had never done to his master in his whole life. He kicked him in the shins.

"*Oww!*"

"Sorry, sire – I tripped. I think we'd better bow."

When the bowing was over, Roger sprang forward and blinked his big, tearful blue eyes. "Your majesties, terrible things have been happening to me – and it's all *their* fault! I'm actually just a poor servant boy who they kidnapped, and then they –"

"We know what has happened," said King Arthur – sorry – *Alf*.

"I'm glad because after they kidnapped me they made me go to this castle and ..."

"We know that you are a Little Horror, and not to be trusted!" added Guinevere – sorry – *Pete*.

Roger now turned his eyes on Sidney Smith. "You mean you'd rather believe a mangy moggy than me, the son of the most powerful knight in the North?"

"Ah! So you *aren't* a poor servant boy!" cried King Alf – sorry – well, you know what I mean by now.

Realising the game was up, Roger stamped past them into Camelot itself. "Wait till my father arrives with his army, you pathetic lot! *He'll* believe me, and then you'll pay for this!"

And he began to stamp around the castle grounds, crying at the top of his voice, "KING ARTHUR IS A STUPID BIG-NOSE!!! GUINEVERE IS AN UGLY OLD FISH-FACE!!!"

"I haven't got a big nose!" Alf complained (but unfortunately, he had).

"I'm not old!" added Pete (which was true).

And as the *real* King Arthur and Queen Guinevere came out to welcome the travellers home, Roger was parading past them yelling, "KING ARTHUR'S GOT A BRAIN THE SIZE OF AN APPLE PIP! SMELLY GUINEVERE NEVER CHANGES HER UNDERWEAR!"

Alf muttered, "It would have to be a big apple, that's all I can say."

Pete kept quiet.

"Now, now," warned the real King Arthur. "What's all this about?"

In reply, Roger stamped on the king's foot, and bit Guinevere's knee. He was promptly

arrested by the guards as he tried to run away.

Alf and Pete were most relieved to get back to their ordinary jobs. They had never realised how stressful being royal could be.

After Sir Gadabout's untimely return, the real king and queen, and most of the rest of Camelot, had been talking about nothing else than the fate of Gads and Co. On discovering what Sir Gadabout and his friends had had to put up with on their long journey, and knowing that Sir Lancelot would soon be able to knock Roger into shape, they threw a little party for them that evening.

"You should have seen the look I gave Lord Stonefist," said Herbert, trying to make himself heard above the hubub of the party. "I could tell he didn't want to tangle with *me!*"

"Of course," said Sir Gadabout, "I had my suspicions about that Little Horror right from the very beginning. I didn't say anything so as not to worry the others."

"Yeah, and I just saw a pig go flying by," said Sidney Smith.

Sir Gadabout looked up. "Ooh – missed it!"

There was still the small matter of the three most powerful armies in the land marching on Camelot. Guinevere dealt with Sir Dexter and Sir Sinistral – she had a way of talking to men. They all went away trying to fit together a variety of fascinating wooden puzzles she had made. (These were actually meant for their children – but the grown-ups had to try them out, you understand.)

Sir Pelligrew the Portly arrived with his men, still thinking that Roger had been kidnapped – but after seeing the armies of the Left and Right off, Guinevere was able to persuade him of the truth about the Little Horror, and she sent him on his way after telling him the one about the vicar and the cheeky monkey, and he laughed so much all the way back that the weatherman spoke of hurricanes over most of Yorkshire that day.

Lord Stonefist was a different matter. He had the strongest army of all, and he was angrier than ever. *But* it turned out that he had realised how peaceful life was without Roger. Odd things had stopped happening. Unexplained wars had stopped breaking out. Loud and rude noises at the breakfast table had ceased. So when it was learned that Lord Stonefist had come only because he had heard a rumour that Roger was to be *returned* to him, he was easily satisfied. In fact, Lord Stonefist was so relieved to hear that Roger was staying at Camelot for a number of years that it *seemed* he shed a tear of joy – but Ernie said it was merely an eyelash stuck in his eye.

The invading Host of the Undead presented a trickier proposition. Merlin had to sort

them out with an Unspell, which whisked them straight back to their forest where they Unlived ever after.

And Sir Percy was almost able to sit down again.

So although everyone knew deep down that Sir Gadabout was still the Worst Knight in the World, it was quite a long time after the party before they mentioned it again.

Also by Martyn Beardsley

Sir Gadabout Gets Worse

When Excalibur is stolen, Gads sets off with his trusty band of followers to find the evil Sir Rudyard the Rancid. They must face the worst if they are to return the mighty sword to its rightful home.

Sir Gadabout and The Ghost

When he sees the ghost of Sir Henry Hirsute, Gads runs up the wall in fright. But soon he's off on another calamitous quest – to clear Sir Henry's name of the ghastly crime of pilchard-stealing.